D1395571

The Ballad of Syd & Morgan

First published in 2018
by Propolis Books
The Book Hive,
53 London Street,
Norwich, NR2 1HL

cover design and art by Niki Medlik
at **studio medlikova**

A CIP record for this book
is available from the British Library

Printed and bound by TJ International, Padstow, Cornwall

www.propolisbooks.co.uk

The Ballad of Syd & MORGAN

Haydn Middleton

propolis

To my beloved Decca

(Oh baby, my hair's on end about you)

The tree rustled.
It had made music
before they were born,
and would continue after
their deaths, but its song
was of the moment.

E M Forster 1910

THE STORY SO FAR

Roger Keith 'Syd' Barrett (1946–2006) grew up in Cambridge, England, where his father was a respected pathologist. He abandoned an art-school diploma course at Camberwell to lead the countercultural band Pink Floyd to mainstream success in 1967, playing a form of psychedelic music that fused experimental rock with sometimes whimsical wordplay. For reasons that are still debated he left the group in spring 1968 to pursue a solo career, but after taking a break from recording, then heading off on a road trip around England, he fetched up back in Cambridge later that same year...

Meanwhile

Edward Morgan Forster OM, CH (1879–1970) was a much-loved English author whose fiction included *Where Angels Fear to Tread*, *A Room with a View* and *A Passage to India*. He was a deft and often mischievously subversive chronicler of Edwardian England, with "Only connect..." (the epigraph to his 1910 novel *Howards End*) summing up his warm humanistic impulse towards understanding and sympathy. He never married, and in 1946 he returned as an honorary fellow to his *alma mater* King's College, Cambridge, a brisk five-minute bicycle ride away from Syd Barrett's home.

He'd known more spectacular autumn Saturdays. The ash-white skies over Cambridgeshire seemed especially cavernous, the sun showing through just to poke out its tongue. And when at last the thin light began to dim, Saturday afternoon's presiding demigod washed and dried his teacup, then he took the opportunity to leaf back through his notes while he waited for his evening counterpart to report, slightly late, for duty.

Slipping between their jurisdictions in the world far below a lean young man with a shaggy black grown-out perm broke at a fast clip up Silver Street from the river, using the centre of the road rather than the pavement, as if to keep the soaring brickwork on either side at a manageable distance.

Every one of the oncoming cyclists, and even the solitary car, took care to swerve out of his way. Straight-backed and flat-footed in his snakeskin boots, there was a high-arched bounce to his walk that few could have mistaken for jauntiness.

Nobody out and about late on that Saturday afternoon even tried to meet the pair of deep violet bullets that were his pupils, but several shoppers heading for home did glance behind once he'd gone by.

A father holding his small daughter's hand flung back a keen-eyed look. A woman in her early twenties frowned as she caught a familiar spoor which she then seemed unable to square with the walker's pallid complexion and swarthily unshaven jaw.

'Syd?' she mouthed.

Even if she had said the name out loud, the Byronic young man returning to cut such a swathe through his native Cambridge might not have answered. He had been christened Roger and that was what his family – the Barretts at the Homerton end of Hills Road – continued to call him; Syd the Beat was just a nickname that had stuck from his largely unfocused mid-teens.

In fact if he'd been minded to stop and talk to anyone he might have said that still being Syd lay at the root of all his current complications, and that resolving them would involve rather more than just asking to be called something different.

At the very top of Silver Street there was a *contretemps*.

A speedy cyclist swept into view dead ahead, hogging the whole of the road: a large rustic-looking man with a goatee beard, absurdly too broad in the beam for the ladies' Pink Witch bike he was pedalling straight towards Syd Barrett.

There was a bell on the bicycle's handlebars but the rider didn't use it. Instead he gave an angry warning shout – a rich though not especially loud baritone cry that hung on the air with a peculiar tunefulness.

With no time to break step Syd had to skip so quickly aside that he all but lost his balance, before circling on the spot in a little clockwise pirouette, and for a moment his world was made to slip off its axis.

Coming to a standstill as the softer hubbub of the street resumed, he looked both north and south at the T-junction with Trumpington Street. To the woman still mouthing his name it may have seemed he had forgotten which direction he'd been intending to take.

Then he veered off to the north and continued to eat up the ground.

It was October 1968 and England was not overly at ease with itself.

Six months earlier the Conservative MP Enoch Powell had raised the spectre of "rivers of blood" if immigrants from the British Commonwealth continued to arrive in such record numbers; homosexuality had only just ceased to be classed as a criminal act in certain closely defined circumstances; even the song topping the charts was Mary Hopkin's *Those Were the Days*, a haunting Russian reminiscence on youthful idealism banned in its original version by Stalin.

Although no longer at his popinjay zenith of the previous year, Syd still wore clothes that caught the eye: a woman's brick-red crushed velvet jacket, pink tie-dyed tee shirt and black tapered jeans where the norm was now to flare.

Chin raised and jaw squared, he so displaced the air that heads continued to turn as the great raffish ice-cream cake of King's College reared up out of the gloaming on the left-hand side of the next wide Parade.

He looked as if he should be known. Some perhaps mistook his scimitar cheekbones for those of the slightly older English actor Terence Stamp. Others may have confused him with Syd's exact contemporary, Ulsterman George Best, who seemed set fair to bestride world football throughout the 1970s after his Wembley heroics in late May had helped Manchester United to win their first European Cup.

But the two divine onlookers, the second a tad breathless upon his arrival, knew exactly who this boy of great beauty was.

And while the deity whose shift was about to end pulled on his mackintosh with only half an eye on developments down below, his successor followed Syd's progress with the closest interest and amusement, watching his step quicken as he stalked right up to the creamy finials, cupolas and crenellations of King's College and then on through its gatehouse, oblivious to the porters behind their glass partition.

Syd slowed only briefly at the approach to the college's sumptuous introduction: a sprawling lawned court, at the centre of which stood an elaborate fountain.

The vast stone-meringue Chapel stood to his right, its pinnacles pointing skyward like a line of waiting moon shots and dwarfing the three other sides of the square, although each of these too rose in places to three storeys in height.

Across the sward from the Chapel stood a more functional early nineteenth-century residential building and at the lawn's edge Syd turned left towards the stepped entrance to its first staircase.

For half a millennium and more King Henry VI's grand medieval seat of learning had echoed to wave upon wave of youth and discourse. Now all was silent save for the click of Syd's Cuban heels on the recently sluiced perimeter flagstones.

He climbed the building's steps two at a time.

A six-footer like himself standing on the shoulders of a man of similar height would hardly have needed to duck to pass beneath the immense portico. The moulding around it peaked into a flattened arch-head just above which an oriel window of even greater width and height projected outward. A single word was stamped on the arch's left-hand pier: "Private"

Inside Syd went.

The unlit vestibule reeked of gas and stale water. He made straight for the wide stairway with its worn stone treads and started his ascent, checking the names painted in white on the dirty old wooden coal bins beside each closed door until he came to a landing with one marked "Forster".

He rapped on the big door and when no answer came he rapped again, harder.

Somewhere higher up in the building a transistor radio was playing: an exuberant male commentator reporting on a Saturday afternoon sports fixture.

Syd gave the door a third knock.

When still it went unanswered he tried the handle. Finding the door unlocked, he opened it a short way and put his head inside.

There was no sign of anyone.

Syd drew his head back out, checked all round himself on the landing, then made the decision to go in and wait.

After shutting the door behind him with a loud click, he paused to recover his breath while fingering a thin gold chain around his neck.

Even though he had ceased all other movement, the air about him still roared and a visible new tension came into his frame, as if only in the act of arriving did he realise where he had been heading all along, and the true momentousness of his mission dawned on him.

He scanned the room with an unblinking stare.

High-ceilinged and well over twenty feet in length, it was not far short of twenty broad. Heavy curtains almost entirely obscured a pair of lofty early Victorian Gothic windows out of which much of the room's heat seemed to be escaping. The only real light was cast by a soft low lamp next to an upright piano. A fainter glow came from a small well-established coal fire.

It was like stepping back sixty years in time to an over-stuffed Edwardian gentleman's sitting room, the kind of accommodation where a suffragette wielding a toffee hammer might very swiftly have been ankle-deep in expensive debris.

Countless books filled a dozen cases of all heights, shapes and qualities of finish while what looked like a converted bedstead towards the centre held a further wealth of morocco-bound volumes.

More books still were stacked on the uncarpeted floor and on an oval walnut dining table along with piles of loose papers and teetering towers of letters, both opened and unopened. Even the more uncluttered surfaces were dotted with any amount of ornamental bric-a-brac.

There were also plenty of pictures for Syd to run his eye over. The room's assertively floral wallpaper was dotted with framed portraits and engravings of gentlefolk in bonnets and cravats, with some landscapes of the Constable kind.

His gaze lingered longest on an image he really hadn't been expecting to find in such a context, directly above a further, inner door.

He took two involuntary steps towards it, taking him on to one of the floor's threadbare Oriental rugs. It was a reproduction of an early work of Picasso: a naked earth-coloured boy leading a horse the colour of a raincloud.

With an agitated sniff Syd thrust a hand into his jacket pocket and pulled out a pack of cigarettes.

Flipping one up between his lips he rummaged in vain in his other pocket for a lighter, finding only the stiffened corpses of a pair of medium-sized cockroaches, both thickly coated with pink nail varnish.

He sniffed more aggressively and a range of the room's smells crowded in: coal dust, damp earth, furniture polish and fried eggs; a hint of domestic rot.

Then at once they all were gone.

He picked his way around a low, lumpy-looking three-seater sofa with a padded rail and halted in front of the hearth.

The open fire in its green-tiled grate was surrounded by a huge oak mantelpiece, carved and dark, with pigeonhole niches containing a variety of ceramic objects, while vases and large beaten-copper plates lined its highest shelf.

With the toe of his boot Syd nudged a coal aside to raise a flicker of flame, then with an easy athleticism he squatted and held out his cigarette until it caught.

He smoked the cigarette down to its filter without standing, most of the time with his head bowed and his eyes closed tight as if to keep physical pain at bay.

'Oh – ' he sighed after flicking the cigarette butt into the orange coals.

The bleakness of the sound ricocheted back off the mantelpiece and washed across the rugs and footstools behind him.

'Oh – '

The sense of his anticlimax at finding the room empty was palpable, like that of the batsman who marches full of determination out to the wicket with the match hanging in the balance, only to discover all six stumps have been drawn for the night.

He raked his fingers through his hair, grabbing a handful near the crown of his head, giving the impression that he was pulling himself back up to his full height by way of it. And only when he turned to face the room again did he see he was not alone.

To Syd's right stood a florally upholstered William Morris fireside armchair that had seen much better days.

Splayed out upon it lay something in the loose shape of a human figure, looking as if it had been dropped down through a trapdoor in the floor of the room above.

The outline of an elderly gentleman soon grew clearer, his lower limbs swaddled in a colourless knitted shawl reaching down as far as the untied laces in a pair of chestnut brogues.

Syd himself looked as if he hadn't seen the sun in weeks. But in those places where the skin of the seated man showed, it seemed almost too pasty to be that of anyone living, yet the regular rise and fall of a substantial belly indicated he was only asleep.

Under a small cloud of thistledown hair his broad, heart-shaped head was bowed forward, foreshortening his bulbous nose, which in turn cast into shadow a ragged little hedgerow of a moustache.

He wore a grey tweed jacket with a blue and white spotted necktie, the knot of which was askew, as was his pair of silver-framed glasses. A book the size of a piece of toast lay shut on his thigh, his left hand resting claw-like near it, a golden signet ring on one of the long upcurving fingers catching the light from the fire.

It was him. It had to be.

E M Forster, English storyteller supreme, treasure to his nation. And here he was in that no man's land where afternoon cedes to evening – snatching forty winks three months shy of the ninetieth birthday he was due to celebrate on New Year's Day 1969, which was five days before the younger man now looming over him would mark his twenty-third.

This pale twitching face could only be that of a man whose life's most salient details had for decades been in the public domain.

The near-sainted E M Forster. E for Edward, M for Morgan, because although in 1879 his parents had registered him as Henry Morgan, in a farcical muddle at the church he'd been baptised in his father's name, Edward Morgan. So E M not H M he remained, his family calling him Morgan to tell him apart from his father, after which all his dearest friends and even his legion of acquaintances used Morgan too, since Morgan Forster was who he had become.

Syd gazed down transfixed.

Fond commentators had likened the old bachelor's prominent nose and receding chin to a large tweedy mole's. But draped across the chair he could have served as a life-model, without the armour, for Tenniel's White Knight in *Through the Looking-Glass* – that gallant old cove who couldn't stop falling off his horse but who'd eventually proved to be the most helpful, or the least unhelpful, of all the characters Alice ran into during her two sets of adventures.

Inside his own personal aura of stale patchouli smoke and crusted sweat Syd flexed his left leg, redistributing a little of his paltry body weight. But he didn't shift his feet and his arms stayed tight to his sides.

The moment lengthened.

The old man and the new continued to present their *tableau vivant*.

From above the discrepancy between them looked too great, like a splicing-together of film footage from opposite ends of their century, or a stage-production photograph of a fiercely attendant Ariel just freed from his evergreen prison by a Prospero exhausted by his magical labours.

Here they slept and stood: sorcerer in prose, enchanter in song – two very white Englishmen nearly seven decades apart in age, two children born of privilege who had nonetheless been unable to simply accept the world as they'd found it; two men given to Dionysian extremes – if only at times extreme inactivity – the elder born soon after Benjamin Disraeli became Prime Minister, the younger in the year the bikini went on sale.

The *tic-tac* of the standing clock in the corner by the piano seemed to grow louder.

A coal slipped in the grate, the fire crackled and sent strong spurts of flame up the chimney.

And as the flat autumnal light dimmed further until finally it died in the small inner court beyond the tall windows, it was easier to sense the wintriness on the air that gusted in from Siberia across the brooding brown landscapes of East Anglia, while the city's own River Cam licked little pieces out of the meadows before flowing on along the back of this very college, then on again into the Great Ouse until dozens of miles later it entered the Wash to be swallowed by the cold North Sea.

Something in the room had changed.

It pulsed to different echoes and up in the clear empyrean the playful demigod of Saturday evening – Pan the inventor of the seven-reed shepherd's pipe is as good a name for him as any – laid a staying hand on his more straitlaced colleague's coatsleeve.

Beneath the backward sweep of his curved horns, Pan aimed a volley of silvery laughter at the scene below – one he had engineered with an inventiveness which formed so unexpected a flipside to his usual indolence – and he lifted his instrument close to his lips in preparation.

A glance from his eyes the colour of wall-moss suggested that what was about to pass between this pair – if not exactly his protégés, then two mavericks whose mercurial talents he had often been happy to nurture – could be worth his colleague's while to stay on for.

Like a breeze bringing rain just before the first spots are felt, the faintest of rushes went across the Cambridge college room but this wind was distinct from the twelve which blow us all.

Then one of the eyelids of the old gentleman in the scuffed and scruffy armchair flickered open.

A clotted noise broke from Morgan Forster's throat.

Expecting to see nothing but his fire within two yards of the soles of his shoes, he gave the most tremendous start on finding a spectral figure appear to rise out of its flames.

'Not you!' he cried. 'After all this time! No! – '

He thrust himself even further back in his chair, flinging up both arms in a helpless *ad hoc* gesture of exorcism, his voice shrill with alarm, tongue furred with sleep, and much of his mind yet to surface from the parallel realm of dreams. His spectacles tumbled off his nose, and as his small book clattered to the floor a strong whiff of camphor escaped him.

Syd Barrett's eyes widened. He opened his mouth but then appeared to freeze.

He moved neither back nor forward, although just before his own moment of seizure he had cocked out his elbows a short way from his sides, giving him the look of a man who was about to sneeze, perform a somersault or pull a pair of guns from invisible holsters – virtually anything except speak.

Quivering, Morgan scrabbled one-handed for the eye-glasses in his lap, blinking furiously, his limp right arm still raised.

When he found them on the shawl he gave a violent shiver before cramming them on to his nose then peering up in panic through splayed fingers, though his focus did not seem to be on his visitor so much as just behind him.

With a sheepish half-smile Syd shook his head.

'I'm so sorry, sir,' he said at last after clearing his throat, 'but somebody told me where I might find you.'

He spoke softly and with extravagant care at the very front of his tightly pursed mouth, delivering the words like a kind of incantation.

'This person,' he went on after a pause, 'he told me you were open to being visited – '

Dreamily he turned to look across at a little cluster of engraved portraits, as if he were still getting a fix on his new surroundings.

'It's about a picture I painted, you see.'

He returned his attention to Morgan.

'I've come about something I painted, a few years ago.'

Each time he said "painted" he seemed to add a quiet emphasis as if to underline a codeword, the verbal equivalent of a rolled-up copy of *The Times* newspaper.

If he meant it that way, it went over Morgan's head. Still almost horizontal in his chair like a sidecar passenger come adrift from his rider, he made a tiny lurch forward from the shoulder. He shook and then tilted his head to show he hadn't even begun to catch the other's drift.

'I really am sorry to intrude,' Syd told him with greater clarity although no more loudly than before. 'It's most irregular, I know, but I think you may be able to help me.'

His tone, flat and dry, gave a first hint of epic despondency.

'I think – well, this person told me – that you may have a painting I once made.'

He gave another brief and bashful half-smile but his gaze passed through Morgan. Then a darker cast came over his features.

'And I think this could represent my last chance.'

At the point of going on, something in Syd's bearing suggested he had just spotted a more profound level still to his predicament.

Falling silent, he thrust a hand into his jacket pocket.

Morgan flinched at the abruptness of his movement before cuffing away the grubby shawl to free up his legs and swung them both around to one side, cupping a hand over his crotch in self-protection.

'I really am sorry, sir,' Syd said again. 'I should've written first – '

He had trained his sombre eyes on an emptied white teacup with a border of wild strawberries placed on the floor to the side of Morgan's chair.

'But the person did think it was you who had bought it.'

His low tenor voice cracked, cut out, then resumed in an even less sing-song way.

'My painting.'

Few would have guessed that in ballrooms, clubs and halls across two continents Syd had been confident enough to hold a tune before crowds often numbered in their high hundreds. His speech was free of any accent save that of the more southerly tranche of England's educated post-war middle class but while he presented so diffidently, he spoke as if he were describing some deep personal catastrophe.

Morgan squinted up, mystified, his eyes still glued to the brick-red jacket's pocket and whatever tool or weapon might at any moment be ripped out of it.

'I'm so sorry,' Syd said yet again, as if prompted by the pattern of leaves inside the teacup to keep repeating himself. 'But I need that painting back.'

Morgan gave no sign of understanding. He had, however, marginally lowered his hand and was blinking up now less frantically.

Whatever old and demanding demon of nightmare he had imagined this to be, to find that all he in fact faced was a marauding hippie with pleasingly regular features may at least have seemed more negotiable. He gathered himself and strung a sentence together:

'Were you here with me,' he asked, his light faltering voice not noticeably plummier than Syd's, 'before I fell into my matinee sleep?'

Syd in turn gave no sign of being able to respond.

There seemed in that moment to be no way forward.

For although they shared so intimate a space – its fuggy draughts electrified by their two very different types of agitation – each seemed quite beyond the other's conversational wavelength.

The clock in the corner ticked on.

What Morgan was seeing can only be guessed as he got back behind the wheel of himself and eased up through the gears. Perhaps no more at first than the mercury blur of Syd's thwarted energy, the shine and the glamour of that.

But his fine old baby-blue eyes were becoming beadier by the moment, the eyes of a hawk in the face of a mole, pushing on ahead to reconnoitre while the rest of him returned more slowly to full consciousness and capacity. And around the eyes of the younger man he must have noted some dark smudges – actually residual crescents of eye-shadow, but for all Morgan knew, left by coal dust.

'Would you be here,' he tried again, a little less tentatively, 'to bring fuel?'

He indicated with his head the space in the tiled fireplace between the scuttle and the plugged-in electric kettle.

'Only I was told by the domestic bursar that I might expect a delivery of logs – '

Before he could finish, Syd stirred himself and interrupted, the words tumbling out in a faster and even more apologetically mournful monotone onto the patch of floor around the teacup:

'What he told me, you see, is that he thought you were there.

'At the pub. Having a sandwich lunch with your son.

'You noticed my painting in the show, he said, and you bought it.'

Finally Morgan let his lifted arm drop down into his lap. He laid his other hand on his sternum to reassure his still-racing heart.

'The *pub*?' he said, perplexed to the point of irritation.

Instead of answering, Syd took a stride forward, dropped to one knee and bowed his head as if offering his shoulder to be dubbed by a sword.

It happened so fast that the man who resembled Lewis Carroll's White Knight barely had time to slam his eyes shut and recoil.

But in the next moment he felt a light tap on his thigh, and when he looked again Syd was standing on the same spot as before – and the small book he had startled Morgan into dropping lay again in his lap.

'I am so very sorry to be troubling you,' Syd murmured one last time.

He removed his hand, empty, from his pocket and placed it high up on his opposite shoulder.

'And of course,' he added, 'what I was told may not have been serious. About you and my painting.

'It could just have been a joke.'

This possibility seemed finally to stop him in his tracks.

After offering Morgan the ghost of a shrug, the right side

of his mouth twitched upward in what promised to be the most rueful little shot at a grin.

Then without any warning at all the sun came out.

A slow and rather marvellous smile stole from Syd's mouth across the rest of his face – soft and open-eyed, showing all his good white teeth. It was almost too disarming: a smile to make a self-styled lesser mortal want to kneel down and offer up his own soul just to fuel it further, yet now it served only to make him look even more forlorn.

A new fullness remained in Syd's cheeks when it faded.

He stared down at his boots as if something inside him was about to give and come spilling out. But when he next spoke it was with more control than before, and even a kind of battered dignity.

'It's probably too late now anyway,' he said.

He bit down on his lip then let it go.

'I think it's gone. I think it's all over.'

Slumping deeper in his chair, Morgan tried to look away at a small vase of crimson leaves on a nearby table. But sunflower-like, his face was drawn back again towards this radiant, heartsore individual.

He tried another tack.

'Forgive me for asking,' he began, 'but would it be money you are waiting for?'

Syd knitted his brow and again looked away, rapt, at the engravings, apparently giving the question all due consideration.

'Money is the last thing,' he eventually murmured with a pigeon-like bob of his head.

'It's money that was probably the original mistake,' he glossed after another lengthy lapse. 'Allowing that transaction to take place.'

He puffed out his cheeks, linking his fingers before him, his elbows drawn in tightly again to his sides. He had done up across his stomach the single pink pearl button to the brick-red jacket which was at least one size too small for him and cut more obviously now to fit a woman's shape.

'That's when it began, you see,' he said to the wall. 'Or one could say that it did.'

At this point Morgan could hold back no longer.

'You will have to speak up!' he all but shouted.

Syd swung his gaze back around to find the old gentleman jabbing a finger at thin air near to his own ear in a waspish charade of deafness.

He nodded down at him. And at last their eyes locked.

'It wasn't meant to turn out the way that it did!' Syd roused himself to go on, projecting his voice in much the same way as the cyclist back on Silver Street and creating much the same sort of reverberation.

'Not any of it! I didn't want to sell anything, let alone find ways to sustain anyone else's livelihood!

'There was never any question in my mind of taking commissions!'

The vehemence he gave to the last three syllables stalled him once again.

He had been opening his eyes wide at random points as he spoke and on two separate occasions he'd batted a hand absently near his dishevelled head as if to disperse a cloud of midges.

But still his eyes drilled into Morgan's. And they had gone through a sea-change: black bullets no longer – no guns anywhere now – but a cleaner, more limpid hazel-brown with green flecks, the eyes of a person in serious jeopardy, if only from himself, which Morgan would have known to be as deep a jeopardy as any.

'So I've got to try to take the path back, sir,' Syd said, returning to his hesitant murmur and touching his neck chain like an amulet.

'Try to put things right. Start again – '

Morgan looked away, newly flustered, for again he'd have known how it is when a young man stops asking questions of life and life starts asking questions of him. He didn't yet have his uninvited guest's full measure, but plainly much was resting on this.

And perhaps he had, after all, woken up to find a demon in his room.

Drawing off his glasses, Morgan folded them into his fist as if what he'd just seen, or even just thought, was imprinted upon them and had to be denied.

He hauled himself forward by his chair arms until his upper body was more or less erect, and shifting his legs back to their original position as an anchor, he pulled the shawl out from under them and sprinkled it onto the floor.

Though his every move was laboriously slow, there was a gracious, almost ceremonial air to them and for all his obvious infirmity of age the command of proceedings had now passed to him.

There was still much more to this man than may have met the eye – the hallowed author whose fiction told not only of Edwardian England but also of temporary escapes from that somewhat stilted world into indefinable realms beyond, the writer about whom a Bloomsbury friend once claimed that Pan showed his cloven hoof in almost everything he wrote.

Lifting his head higher, Morgan wetted first his upper lip with the tip of his tongue then the fleshier lower one and he tried, though not too hard, to suppress a grimace as he ran a finger along the wattled skin just inside his shirt collar.

'Peering up at you like this is giving me neck ache,' he pretended to grumble.

With chivalrous impatience he waved at a second William Morris chair that stood just a few feet away, angled like his own towards the hearth.

'Would you please sit?' Morgan Forster asked Syd Barrett.

'Sit by me here, and try to explain the difficulty you are in.

'From the beginning.'

Syd took the two steps sooner than Morgan might have expected.

Keeping his back as straight as a dart, he lowered himself warily onto the edge of the chair as if taking his place before a keyboard. Then with the joint of his right thumb he began to describe very small circles on the thigh of his jeans.

When it became clear he wasn't going to start speaking of his own accord, Morgan made a tiny purposeful sound in the back of his throat.

'Now then,' he said. 'You are telling me that you are an artist?'

Syd stared straight ahead at the fire.

'Oh no, I did paint. But I was only ever an art student.'

'So you studied. And where would this have been?'

Syd paused before answering.

'London.'

He raised his line of vision to the huge mantelpiece.

'Camberwell.'

Morgan bowed his head.

'And the show you have mentioned was there?'

'It – No, it was here. Near here. Four years ago. I would have been, well, eighteen.'

He darted a sidelong glance at Morgan, as if to confirm he wasn't just talking to himself, that this most climactic of interviews really was taking place.

'I was still at home. Before I left for college.'

'So Cambridge is your place of origin?'

Syd gave a faraway nod. It looked less like an answer than an acknowledgement of the elegantly simple long-necked white vase, some nine inches in height, which stood in one of the mantelpiece's upper side niches.

Morgan waited in vain for him to say more.

'And you spoke of a pub?'

'Yes sir,' replied Syd with firmness, sitting even straighter. 'The show was in a pub room, out Milton way. My own work and a friend's. Figurative things mainly. Some in oil. Several, I believe, were of bicycles – '

Morgan watched his profile, perhaps in case it should be lit up again by that intoxicating smile, but Syd's expression stayed impassive.

'I'm afraid, sir, that I can't say for certain, now, which pub it was.'

His admission sounded so crestfallen, and the hush which then descended was so similar to the silence that follows a heavy fall of snow, that Morgan made a dismissive gesture suggesting this was the merest technicality.

Syd didn't notice. All his attention was on the mantelpiece. He could have been compiling a mental inventory of all the decorative pieces.

'But one of my paintings was sold. I do know that.'

'A painting of a bicycle?'

'It probably – '

He checked himself.

'Yes, it could very well have been.'

'You are not certain?'

'No, I'm afraid – No, it was a long time ago, sir.'

'You said four years.'

Gently Syd puffed out his cheeks then exhaled.

'Quite a lot has happened in the meantime.'

Morgan looked hard at him then quickly brushed some lint off his sleeve in sympathy.

'My own short-term memory is also far from what it was.'

His powers of hearing, by contrast, had come on in leaps and bounds during the past few minutes. Nothing Syd now said, however softly, needed amplification. Unless the older man had earlier been pretending to be deafer than he really was, it was as if his ears had somehow been tuned to a new frequency.

Syd turned his face Morgan's way and both his eyes were shut, as if he could not bear to see his *de facto* host shake his head in response to whatever he was about to ask next.

Syd's features were death mask serene, yet seated there so stiffly his tall slight body seemed tensed to such a pitch that if he'd been a string on his own Fender Esquire guitar – self-adorned with silver discs to reflect the liquid lights in which his group's otherworldly live shows had been immersed – and somebody had plucked him, the note would surely have shattered every last pot he had just appeared to be committing to memory.

'And if you don't mind, sir,' Syd said, 'I should very much like to have it back now.

'My painting.

'That is – if you have it?'

When he opened his eyes he found Morgan sitting further forward, resting his leather-patched elbows on the chair arms.

He had pressed his fingertips together a short way from his mouth, forming not so much a steeple as what might have served as a protective cage for a weak candle flame.

His glasses, which he hadn't put back on since making his first close inspection of Syd, poked out of his breast pocket while thoughtfully he looked into the fire.

His face was a picture of concentration, the face of a man who knew that after nearly ninety years of wear and tear he had to exert the utmost effort just to stay lucid.

'Leaving aside for a moment the question of whether I have this item,' he said, 'may I ask why its tracking down is of such importance to you?'

Syd continued to draw circles on his thigh, digging in harder with his thumb.

'It was a mistake,' was all he replied in his ominous self-deprecating monotone.

'To have made the painting or to have had it sold?'

Syd didn't reply to that, so Morgan repeated his question. He had taken his glasses from his pocket and begun to polish them with a corner of the shawl he'd retrieved from the floor.

Syd finally allowed some slack into his posture and let both his arms dangle down between his knees. The chair was so low that his knuckles almost scraped the rug.

All his energy seemed to be leaving him.

'I got myself onto the wrong path,' he said.

'And it all started – Well, the way I've come to see it – looking back – is that it all started with that show. So I need to get my painting back.

'Naturally I'm fully prepared to pay for it, and – '

'And then what?' Morgan surprised him by interrupting.

'I beg your pardon?'

'Should you recover this painting, what will then happen? What would you do with it?'

The question caught Syd on the hop.

His hand fluttered up to his neck chain.

'Oh – ' he began. 'Oh, I might very well destroy it.'

'And you believe that such a gesture would "put things right", as you phrased it?'

Syd dipped his nearer hand into his jacket pocket then left it there. He couldn't or wouldn't give any other answer. But the old man seemed temporarily satisfied.

'And does this painting carry a signature?'

'Oh, I – Well, I don't quite – It may be signed, yes.'

'In which name would that be?'

Considering his reply, Syd moved his hand around inside his pocket.

'Well, from that period, it may possibly just say "Syd".'

Briefly some colour flared in his cheeks.

'That is your name?'

Very cautiously Syd drew his cigarette pack out of the pocket, as if he didn't want Morgan, who was still rubbing away at his glasses, to notice.

'It's a name that I've used.'

'Would that be as in "El Cid" – or "Le Cid" as Corneille had it?' Morgan paused in his rubbing. 'There is no accounting for parental choice,' he added, 'but I should not have had you down for a Sidney.'

A muscle by Syd's mouth twitched. Suddenly he looked so tired that he could have been about to yawn. Then quickly he went on, his voice faint and drained of hope.

'But what I'd do with the painting isn't really the issue, sir. As I said, it could well be too late now anyway. And besides,' he sent a fearful look Morgan's way, 'it may not have been you at all that day? In the pub?'

Morgan finished polishing his glasses and eased them back on. Syd looked directly at him and Morgan held his hungry gaze with an answering hunger. As he searched Syd's face he raised his palms.

'My dear boy,' he replied, 'I have not yet said I am not your man. But if you will allow it, may I enquire: is the painting really all you have come here for?'

Again Syd's colour rose.

He let his gaze drop to his lap where the sight of the cigarette pack seemed to startle him.

'Is it all right if I smoke?' he asked.

Morgan gestured that he was welcome, and when Syd leaned across to offer the opened pack to the older man, he touched his fingertips to his pouchy cheek, weighing up his options.

'No I shan't,' he finally decided. 'You have only two left.'

Syd waved away his concern by pushing the pack closer,

moving it up and down as an inducement.

Morgan sat back and shook his head with a smile.

'Maybe later.'

Syd rose, then got down again on his haunches in front of the fire.

After catching his light and before standing, he ran a hand down one of the mantelpiece's shallow bevelled recesses. Once back on his feet, taking care not to seem to be reading any of Morgan's creamy invitation cards with their cursive black lettering, he appraised the five neatly turned twelve-inch-high supporting columns which ran between the top two shelves of the elaborate construction.

'That piece of furniture does rather tend to dominate,' Morgan admitted.

'It was designed by my father in the 1870s, and has followed me around from one room to another all my life!'

Drawing on his cigarette, Syd nodded as he turned to face him.

'My father was an architect, d'you see,' Morgan went on, watching Syd's smoke coil up into the shadows of the ceiling.

'Not that he was given much time to practise after his student days. He died before I was two years old – consumption – so for me that piece has all the more value. Sentimental, if not strictly aesthetic'

Just as Syd had earlier laid so strong an emphasis on the word "painted", now Morgan twice put unexpected stress on "father", and if any reaction from Syd the first time was hard to pick up, a brief but distinct quickening of interest was there in his eyes at the second, as it was again at the word "died".

Instead of commenting though, he looked about him for an ashtray before re-settling in the chair.

Morgan reached down to pat the floor until he found his teacup and held it up.

'Oh no, I really don't think – ' said Syd, doubtless having noted the cup's delicacy.

'Please,' Morgan insisted. 'Take it. Like the mantelpiece, it is here to be used.'

He showed his upper row of dentures in an amiable little smile.

'We all of us are.'

Morgan leaned forward to tie both his shoelaces and tucked himself back into the chair beneath his shawl.

Now that he had fully and finally emerged from his afternoon nap, his foggy-coloured hair looked less unruly, and more than a dash of flamboyance was coming into each of his leisurely movements.

'This painting of yours?' he began again.

Syd gave a nod at the cup he had begun to line with ash.

'You say it was of a bicycle?'

'Very possibly.'

Syd narrowed his eyes in an attempt at recollection.

'Though,' he went on, 'it could have been an insect.'

He turned his face to Morgan.

'Or even a number of insects.

'Flies, and so on.'

Closer to, the young man's ashen skin looked a yet more livid nocturnal shade of ivory, its default lack of expression quite possibly caused by crushing fatigue. But still his flat-planed face in the firelight was compelling; despite the dark stubble it could have come straight out of the Bayeux Tapestry, and if Morgan had reached out to touch it he might have taken care not to pull a thread.

'You have given me surprisingly little to go on,' Morgan said with interest rather than as a criticism.

'Both as regards your picture's subject, and the place where it was shown. Have you perhaps had quite a number of exhibitions?'

Syd exhaled a tidy jet of smoke.

'No, just one.'

Morgan nodded.

'Then you are in good company. As you will probably be aware, the great Blake held a single exhibition, at least within his own lifetime. And he sold a solitary work!'

Syd looked mildly shocked.

'William Blake? Oh no, I was never in his sort of league.'

Morgan digested this, then under his breath he gave an odd little whoop.

'Well, that may be all to the good,' he declared. 'As I recall it, a reviewer at the time dismissed poor Blake's only show as "the work of an unfortunate lunatic"!'

Syd swung his head away to the door he'd come in through.

He had begun again the circling on his thigh, now with the half-crown-sized base of the teacup.

'But like Blake,' said Syd, 'I'm fairly sure I only ever did sell one work.'

'Oh – '

Morgan paused.

'Oh, I see. And you are now of the opinion that this was one too many?'

*

'The man who directed you here,' said Morgan, to end the long silence which greeted his last remark, 'is he a person you know well?'

Syd shook his head and muttered something Morgan didn't quite catch.

He eased forward, cupping his ear. 'Say again?'

'It was just someone at the BBC,' Syd repeated. 'Someone I met one of the times I was there. It must have been about a year ago.'

He gnawed at his lip.

'And no, I didn't know him well. An older man, he was.

'He just told me he happened to be at the pub too. You know – when the exhibition was on?'

'The BBC,' said Morgan neutrally. 'What were you doing there?'

Syd took a last draw on his cigarette and half-winced, half-smiled, as rather tenderly he ground out its stub against the inner base of the teacup.

'Wasting everyone's time, as it turned out.'

He set the cup down on the floor by his boot.

'Including my own.'

Morgan wasn't yet ready to let this go.

'You worked at the BBC?'

He couldn't help sounding amused by the idea of Syd playing a role of any kind at an institution where even by the late 1960s, despite a certain amount of reordering on the radio side, most people still sported ties and short-back-and-sides haircuts.

'Would this have been after you graduated from your school of art?'

'No,' Syd replied, his hands – as long-fingered as Morgan's own – clapped to his knees as if he were about to rise.

'No?' asked Morgan.

'I wasn't – Well, I didn't stay at Camberwell right through to graduation.'

'You left to work at the BBC?'

'No!'

The room echoed to a faint new petulance but the plaintive look Syd at once threw Morgan's way showed it was only self-directed.

'I left my course to do something else. Something which didn't in the end come to fruition.'

Morgan eyed him.

'I should be interested to know what that was.'

'No,' Syd replied fast, clearly having anticipated the question.

'No, that's definitely gone now. That ship has sailed.'

He cast a longing look around himself, at the massed pieces of furniture and decoration that could almost have been peering back at him through the subdued light, crouched and vigilant.

And amid all the examples of human craftsmanship and artistry on show there was definitely something of the animal world, too, about Morgan Forster's crucible of a room – warren, burrow, cocoon – something perhaps in the now slower, earthier play of its air. Even a man not already as shattered as Syd might have found himself seduced into seeing it as a capsule that had drifted free from its everyday moorings, inviting him simply to curl up and be restored by sleep.

'Look,' he was moved to continue by a cooler draught that came from the direction of one of the windows, 'there's nothing left. Not now.

'There was something once.'

He waved a listless arm.

'First there was nothing, then I had something – for a very short while – but now there's nothing again. It's gone.'

He took a breath.

'I think I must have made it go.'

'But if you no longer study,' asked Morgan, 'nor do you have anything to do with the BBC, then an able-bodied young person like yourself must surely do something with his time?'

Syd's bullet eyes glittered.

'Sir,' he all but shouted, 'I do nothing!'

'Not any more,' he went on, instantly mortified at having raised his voice.

'That's why I'm here. To see if I can go back and start again, but on a different path. The path I should have stayed on.'

From under his brow he looked at Morgan in supplication.

No one with Syd's bone structure could ever have looked truly hangdog but this was as close as it came.

Morgan refused to look back, the epitome of a man who deplored incivility of any kind and was prepared to tell the world so; a man who for that very reason once figured on a list drawn up by Joseph Goebbels of all the Britons who faced annihilation in the event of a Nazi conquest.

'And I'm taking up so much of your time,' Syd pleaded, 'when all I need to know is whether it actually was you? There in the pub that day, buying my painting?'

The old gentleman bowed his head then he foxed Syd by setting aside his shawl and heaving himself up on to his feet.

An inch of thick oatmeal sock showed between his shoes and his slightly too short trousers, which could now be seen to match the grey tweed of his jacket.

He seemed able to stand steadily enough unaided and he was corpulent, yet there looked to be no great weight to him, as if his substantial torso might be made up at least in part of puffed-out plumage.

'One thing I can tell you with certainty about that day,' he said a little caustically to Syd who had risen to his own feet and awaited the punchline with bated breath, 'is that I was not lunching – upon sandwiches or anything else – with my son.'

'Oh – ' Syd began.

'It has never fallen to me to be a father,' Morgan overrode his visitor.

For a third time he said "father" as if italicising the word and while Syd registered this with a wide-eyed look, the more peculiar part was that Morgan himself seemed surprised at how he'd just heard himself speak.

He ran his tongue around the inside of his mouth almost as if to check where the words had come from.

'I am afraid you will now have to excuse me for a short while,' he announced.

Syd took a step back to let him pass – unnecessarily, since Morgan was already heading in a halting but determined shuffle towards the doorway to the landing.

There was a moment of muddle at the door, which Syd had loped across the room to open inwards for his host.

Morgan did not immediately step across the threshold, maybe because he wasn't keen for a stranger to stay behind with all his belongings.

So Syd himself stepped out onto the unlit landing. Only then did it become apparent how much warmer and more congenial that firelit crucible of a room had been.

'I'll – ' Syd stammered. 'Shall I wait for you out here, then?'

But he wasn't quite far out enough and he appeared to be positioning himself to block Morgan's exit.

The old gentleman, who had been a six-footer before age rounded his shoulders into a stoop, tilted up his head to search the younger man's face.

'I mean,' Syd struggled on, evidently concerned that if Morgan disappeared from view he might never return, 'would you prefer me to come with you?'

Morgan gave a restless little shake of the head.

After even so short a period of intensity he perhaps needed some time apart to gather himself. He could, on the other hand, have been on his way to a bathroom, although he might just as easily have been about to fetch a pair of college servants to frogmarch Syd off the premises.

'Are you perhaps,' Syd managed to ask, visibly excruciated, 'going to fetch my painting?'

'This is my home,' Morgan replied in a low, steadfast voice, 'so I see no need to account for my movements.

'But since you ask, I have medications to take. Such is the lot of the expensively preserved near-nonagenarian.

'Now would you please step aside?'

Syd obeyed, and Morgan toiled past him in the direction of a set of stone steps which led up to another door. It was very dark indeed on the landing, and there seemed to be no light switch on the wall.

Syd went after him.

At the foot of the first step, he threw caution to the wind, reached out and put a hand on the old man's elbow.

Quailing, Morgan began slowly to turn.

Syd dug a fist deep into the hip pocket of his jeans and after rummaging around he pulled out a crinkled ball of high-denomination banknotes which he proffered on his palm.

'I'm not asking you for any favours,' he said.

'To get my picture back, I'm willing to pay much more than it cost. Much more than it's worth.'

Morgan may have been unable to see what was being shown but he made no closer inspection nor did he attempt to move on. Syd crammed the money back into his jeans then reached into one after another of his jacket's inner pockets.

'I have a cheque book,' he said, although it seemed he

could not at that precise moment lay a hand on it.

'I'm prepared to go as high as you like.'

'Look here,' said Morgan without raising his eyes and sounding both resigned and peeved. 'I really will not be very long.

'Occupy yourself for a while. Smoke your last cigarette, why don't you?'

He clicked his tongue and Syd took a cowed step back.

Morgan went on up the steps and finding the door ajar, he passed through to an even darker space before pulling it up behind him and locking it.

From somewhere up the next main flight of stairs the transistor radio played on: an announcer with a sepulchral voice reading the afternoon's classified football results.

Instead of returning to Morgan Forster's room, Syd leaned back against the landing wall and appeared to give every ounce of his attention to the litany of West Bromwich Albions, Sheffield Wednesdays and Crystal Palaces through to Bournemouth and Boscombe Athletics and Workingtons.

He may, as he listened, have been noting which locations he had careered through on his recent extended break from London's recording studios, chauffeuring a pair of high-octane old Cambridge friends around the country in his Austin Mini.

Or he could have been associating placenames with dank municipal venues where The Pink Floyd had performed their increasingly cheerless thirty-minute concerts – nearly two hundred of them in 1967 alone – the wild intergalactic racket that mushroomed up out of Syd's radical improvisations on lead guitar at times provoking physical assault from fans who craved faithful retreads of the group's small handful of hits.

But when the invocation of this particular sporting England was complete he pushed himself back off the wall and flexed his shoulders as if he really were emerging from a period of communal prayer.

Morgan had yet to reappear.

Syd gave a long, luxuriant, despairing yawn.

He produced his pack of cigarettes, opened it, but closed it again without tapping the last one out.

Then he walked over to the zigzag stairway he had come up earlier and gazed down through the banister rails into swirling darkness: so many steps for a man of Morgan's age and condition to have to mount on a regular basis.

After that, he looked into the deeper dark above.

The sound of the radio may have been coming from rooms used before the Great War by another young man with the initials R B who also came soon to success and was touted as the handsomest in England. Rupert Brooke had not been an exact contemporary of Morgan's but they were friendly enough to be on Christian-name terms. Six decades earlier they may well have stood amusing each other on this very spot.

Syd took a couple of paces towards the door Morgan had shut behind him.

Around its perimeter a faint yellow light now showed, though no sounds came.

He checked his step, yawned once more, then looked back

at the inviting hearth through the sitting room's doorway, and the William Morris chair which, while out at the elbows, had been a good deal more comfortable than the driver's seat in the Mini he had so recently run aground, its petrol tank empty, down by the river.

And the illustrious author had not, after all, specifically requested him to wait out in the cold and dark for his return.

Back in the room, leaving the door fully open, Syd went first to the hearth and stood ramrod straight with his back to the fire, warming his calves and lower thighs.

After a further series of yawns, his right shoulder dipped and his posture became altogether more *louche* but still he didn't sit. Perhaps he knew that once back in the chair he might struggle to stay awake.

Instead he picked a path between the furniture to a high window, in front of which stood a simple desk with a high-backed chair tucked underneath.

It wasn't the mess of paperwork that had caught his eye. Nor was it the pile of old sepia photographs, topped by a young moustachioed man got up in subcontinental garb which Syd may have failed to identify as a 1920s image of Morgan himself.

With his thumbs hooked into his hip pockets he bent forward at the waist to get a closer look at a small object standing by the switched-off lamp.

It was a miniature green-painted budgerigar with a patch of red on each wing and barred yellow legs. There was something very sure in its execution. Almost anything in the room would have repaid close scrutiny but this particular piece had called across to Syd.

Swaying a little at the hips, after inspecting it for some while from above he skirted the desk's corner and stooped lower to see it from another angle. In so doing he noticed a large, drably coloured but nicely marbled nocturnal moth at rest on the long red curtain.

As if all these observations gave him the right at last to take the weight off his feet he returned to reposition himself in the fireside chair, not merely perching this time but nestling back into its surprisingly pliant upholstery.

Soon he was unable to prevent his shaggy head from flopping to the side against one of its wings.

Still Morgan Forster did not come.

Syd folded one hand over the other in his lap, the way Morgan's hands were arranged as he had slept. His eyelids then dropped as if in obedient response to the lightest touch from fingers above.

Within three minutes his breathing was that of a man out for the count.

Morgan paused in the room's doorway at his return.

He raised his head and seemed to sniff at the air for fresh cigarette smoke, or perhaps he had just been alerted to the moth fluttering up into a new position on the curtain.

His hair had been dampened down and combed across the top of his domed forehead, his tie was no longer quite so skew-whiff and he stood just a little taller, so that now behind his circular glasses he might have passed in the dimness for Heinrich Himmler's benign older brother.

But he brought no painting with him.

Deducing from Syd's position in the armchair that he must be asleep, Morgan pulled the door softly to behind him but did not try to shut it for fear of its loud click.

Already light on his feet, he did not have to make a special effort to tiptoe back to the fireside. At the grate he paid himself forward stage by stage until he was able to pick up a small brass poker.

He stirred the coals a little but tipped on no fresh cobbles from the scuttle, again not wanting to disturb his visitor. If his personal share of a new load of seasoned timber recently gifted to the college had been delivered as promised then he could have wedged on a log without making too much commotion, but that was not to be.

He straightened up, turned, glanced across at a two-bar electric heater and decided the room's temperature did not yet warrant using it.

With the backs of his legs to the fire's thin warmth, Morgan looked the seated sleeper up and down, and might then have breathed like Shakespeare's Miranda, 'Oh brave new world, That has such people in't!' Yet the character from *The Tempest* whom Morgan still more closely resembled was Miranda's far worldlier father Prospero – and like that displaced duke, he could hardly have reached so late a stage in life without a saucerful of secrets all his own.

Something here, however, must have seemed new even to him.

Syd's long legs were stretched out straight in front of him, crossing at the ankles, and through a large hole in the sole of his right boot, around the ball of his foot, some dirt-streaked skin showed through. There were flecks too of mud, or possibly dark paint, on the shins of his jeans.

His folded hands looked by contrast pristine, perhaps more cared-for than any other part of him, the short squared-off nails manicured not bitten, and luminously clean.

As well as poets like Rupert Brooke, and naturally countless other writers of all stripes from A E Housman and T S Eliot to Henry James and Gore Vidal, Morgan had been in the company of a fair few painters in his time and the hands of none would have looked like these.

Like a judge in a game of musical statues he moved his head from side to side, leaning forward and placing his hands on the fronts of his thighs to study Syd more closely as on he sailed through sleep, his chiselled face tortoiseshell-blank.

But what Morgan had also never seen before was anyone weeping in silence while they slept. For tears were now glistening on both Syd Barrett's cheeks.

As if he had tried to apply drops to his eyes and just missed, clear rivulets snaked from their outer corners, around his prominent cheekbones then down past his not quite parted lips. They seemed to be drying, but just to make sure the White Knight in his grey tweed suit took a single breathless step forward, his heart so snagged that he touched a liver-spotted hand to his own cheek.

He took just one step since a second then proved beyond him.

For a moment it looked as if he might not be able to stay on his feet at all without support, and no piece of furniture was now close enough for him to grab on to.

Morgan's hand slid from his cheek to his neck as his head sagged even further forward, then he listed over to his left, leading him into a short stagger by means of which he mercifully managed to right himself.

His last few years had been peppered with minor strokes, falls, breakages, but this had not been one of those.

His eyes stayed shut for the brief seizure's duration.

On reopening them he was alerted to new activity.

If Morgan had not been facing into the room, with the door in his peripheral vision, he might not have noticed.

His ears certainly had not picked up the preceding taps from outside, little more than a light scratching made by someone who had doubtless been instructed not to knock too hard in case the eminent resident fellow should be indisposed.

Now, though, as the newcomer's head hoved into view around the side of the open door, Morgan's attention was caught.

In fact he became aware of a new presence sooner than he himself was spotted among the room's flickering shadows.

So when this second tall and wiry young man – patchily bearded, still perhaps adolescent, very possibly an occasional weekend worker on the college's garden staff – finally zeroed in on him and made to explain himself, Morgan was able to put a finger to his lips then indicate, by shuffling stiff-legged towards him while genially shooing him back with both arms, that they would have to talk out on the landing.

Once again outside, and having pulled up the door within an inch of closure, Morgan greeted his new visitor with a smile that was inquisitive until he saw two wicker baskets full of hardwood logs no bigger than a man's hand.

'Oh!' he exclaimed, pointing at them with pleasure. 'Oh now – '

But the lad, dressed from head to ankle in navy denim and with his tarnished-gold hair dragged back in a ponytail from his narrow face, was thrusting at Morgan what looked like a small discoloured letter of introduction, his free hand clenched valet style at the small of his back.

On taking it from him, Morgan realised it was a relatively rare £20 note.

'It was out here on the floor, Professor,' the lad explained in his Fenland drawl.

'Oh – ' said Morgan for a third time. 'Yes, I think I know who may have dropped this.'

The lad's prominent Adam's apple bobbed.

'I just found it, Professor,' he went on, forestalling any accusation.

In contrast to the way both Morgan and Syd spoke, the sound of his words was scratchy, blurred, as if there were dust on his needle.

'Yes, yes, thank you so much,' said Morgan, and he looked up.

'You may leave it with me, and if it does not belong to the gentleman who is at present calling on me, I shall make other enquiries on the staircase.'

He curled up the note in one hand and gestured at the baskets.

'I see too that you have brought me winter fuel. Well done again.

'Now, if you would be so good as to leave one of the baskets out here by the coal bin, then the other might be taken into my room and left by the fire-irons?'

Even before Morgan finished speaking the lad was nudging back the first basket with his foot to the bin's side and picking up the second.

'But would you please take care not to disturb my guest beside the fire?'

Saying nothing, the lad waited for Morgan to step back into the room and hold the door open for him, then through he went.

Although Morgan was no longer an active member of the Garden Committee – his sole official college post since returning to King's, and some complained he had been none too active even there – he still took an interest in whatever he saw on his short daily walks and he felt certain he had seen this rather unfinished-looking lad out on the college grounds.

He wore plimsolls and trod stealthily so there was no threat of him rousing Syd before he set down the basket.

He might not even have bothered to look at Morgan's guest before turning to leave. But when by chance he did, if Morgan's hearing had been more acute, he might have heard the lad's jaw drop.

Morgan certainly didn't miss the smile as fresh as paint that flashed across his face when he paused and did a double-take.

And while he didn't mouth Syd's pseudonym quite as expressly as the young woman had on Silver Street, his lips did appear silently to form the shape of his surname too.

He looked around himself, incredulous, as if the rest of The Pink Floyd – or even a lesser Beatle, or a Kink – might also be about to appear.

Then he saw Morgan in the doorway busily beckoning to him and with a final stupefied look down at the equivalent for him of one of William Blake's angels made manifest, he walked on.

‘My guest is known to you?’ asked Morgan *sotto voce*, pulling the outer door to as soon as the lad passed back onto the landing.

‘Well – ’ he replied. ‘Yes – ’

His voice was now hushed as well as blurred, his face flushing so ferocious a shade of red that alongside his navy denim he was two-thirds of the way to completing the colour combination of the Union Jack.

Keeping one hand on the door’s handle for support, with an encouraging dip of the head Morgan invited him to go on.

‘Well, Professor,’ he said, ‘that’s Syd Barrett.’

Morgan craned his neck forward, inclining his right ear to hear still more.

The lad delayed his reply by wiping bark dust off his palms onto his shirt in the region of his ribcage.

‘And he’s – you know? – a god.’

As if remembering himself Morgan smiled and reached into his trouser pocket.

‘My dear chap,’ he said as he rooted about, ‘you really must stop calling me Professor. I am no more a Professor than I am a professional golfer.’

He studied the handful of change he'd found, put it back, then produced instead from his jacket a ten-shilling note which he pressed on the speechless youth.

'For bringing up the logs,' he said. 'And for your straight-dealing over turning in the larger note.'

He leaned in again, mock-conspiratorially.

'Now, we have here a Mr Barrett, you say? And how is it that you know him?'

The lad looked baffled.

'The way everyone does, sir. From the music.'

'Music?'

'The records.'

'Gramophone records? We are talking about popular music? "Pop"?'

'The stuff he did with his group, sir? The Pink Floyd. Spaced-out music. Psychedelic?'

'Psychedelic? Oh my word!'

'With all the amazing light shows and projections? It was him who started all of that.'

He searched for a better way to express himself.

'The shadows and the bubbling colours and stuff, you know, when they did the music live? Kind of mind-expanding. Getting you to see things different? More, like, real?'

The lad's questions were not necessarily rhetorical. He seemed unsure as to whether this was some kind of an initiation test or if the old gentleman really did need a few hard facts about the singer and guitarist who had cried himself to sleep in his sitting room.

'*I've got a bike, you can ride it if you like*?' the lad quoted dubiously with a closer look at Morgan.

'Is that so?' Morgan answered, flummoxed. 'Ah, well I really – '

'*The Piper at the Gates of Dawn*?'

Morgan's eyes widened.

'What's that you say?'

'*The Piper at the Gates of Dawn*. That was their LP – The Pink Floyd's. When Syd – I mean – when Mr Barrett was still with them? Before he went solo?'

Morgan smiled.

'Oh! Now that is intriguing.'

He nodded and the lad, for want of a more appropriate response, nodded back.

'So he is no longer with this – group?' Morgan asked.

The lad shook his head, a version of his earlier smile returning.

'That really is most helpful,' said Morgan. 'Thank you so much.'

The lad's smile curdled in non-committal reply and plainly though Morgan had dismissed him, equally plainly he was not yet ready to go.

'There was this too, sir,' he mumbled.

He had reached in and taken something small and off-white from the unfastened breast pocket of his overshirt. It could have been another crumpled note of even higher denomination.

'It was down on the ground,' he explained. 'By the money.'

He offered it on the palm of his hand to Morgan: a

straightened-out, quite substantial clarion-shaped cannabis joint, darkening from fawn to a greasy ash-black at the end where it had earlier been extinguished.

'I didn't know if I should just – ' the lad began with a guilty shrug.

He nodded past Morgan at his sleeping idol.

'But seeing as how it probably, like, belongs to him as well – ?'

He ran dry.

'You wish me to give this cigarette to Mr Barrett too?' asked Morgan.

The lad nodded, passed it across, and with a strange little geisha-style bow he slid away to the top of the flight of stairs then was gone.

Back in the room Morgan did manage to close the door without too resounding a click.

He placed the joint with the £20 note inside a mantelpiece niche where there was also, had Syd looked harder before, a small box of matches for lighting the fire.

Turning then, he took the discarded shawl from his chair, opened it out and lightly draped it over the collapsed young star.

From there Morgan pottered into the deeper recesses of his room, picking up the small novel of George Meredith's he had been reading and setting it down on a table. Again he seemed to be trying to detect something on the air, and cast a faintly concerned look at the windows.

Next to a glass-fronted bureau he switched on an architect's white lamp on a hinged arm – assertively modern-looking amid so much Edwardiana – and at once its bright light picked out a pattern of swirls in the old floor rug beneath it.

Then he unlocked the bureau doors with a key that was already in place and after opening them outward he examined a line of books until he found the one he wanted.

The volume, dating back to the century's opening decade and bound in bottle-green, was no larger than one of the logs Morgan had just had delivered. He opened it at its dark blue frontispiece which showed three cherubic children at a small waterfall, with a naturalistic otter in the foreground among reeds.

And a River went out of Eden, ran its caption.

He leafed forward to check the contents page and, apparently satisfied, closed up the bureau, switched off the lamp, then made his way back to the armchair where Syd Barrett – in the wake of a colossal silent yawn – was about to re-enter the land of the living.

Morgan stayed out of Syd's line of vision as deftly he balanced the green book on the arm of the young musician's chair then took two steps back to his own seat.

Syd sat forward and looked around the room.

His eyes seemed to struggle to find a point of purchase and he hadn't yet seen that Morgan had returned. But after managing to orient himself, he relaxed sufficiently to yawn again, more modestly this time, lowering his head and raising the back of one hand half way to his mouth.

It was then that he noticed the shawl, which after a moment he peeled off his lap, and in so doing his eye fell upon the little green book.

'Something you may be interested in,' said Morgan.

Syd followed the voice to its source and seemed momentarily not to recognise the freshly spruced up old gentleman whose teeth were now showing in a small shy smile.

'I'm sorry – ' Syd began. 'I rather think I must have – '

'The book,' Morgan elaborated with a playful open-handed gesture. 'I looked it out for you. Why don't you see what it is?'

Syd picked it up as if it might be about to explode.

Holding the spine towards the fire he arched his neck to read the title's embossed lettering then he looked back at Morgan.

'It is a first edition,' his host told him. 'American, from 1908. As you will see, it is unillustrated.'

He made it sound as if Syd might throw a tantrum at finding no pictures. But Syd, having read no more than the title, continued to fix Morgan with his expressionless stare.

'Please,' Morgan urged him. 'Do look inside.'

He paused.

'I believe that chapter seven is of the most immediate relevance?'

Syd had no need to open the book and turn to that chapter. And his stare, not quite challenging but not completely bewildered either, implied that Morgan was already well aware of this.

The book in Syd's hands was Kenneth Grahame's anthropomorphic fantasy for children *The Wind in the Willows*, its centrepiece seventh chapter describing a mystical night excursion taken by Rat and Mole in search of the missing young son of Otter: a chapter entitled *The Piper at the Gates of Dawn*.

Morgan's smile became more inscrutable. He glanced over at the standing clock.

'Now I am not much of a drinking man,' he conceded, 'but in that low cupboard you will find a decanter of what I regard as some passable sherry, with glasses.'

He had winched himself around in his armchair to point across the room, with one eye closed for greater accuracy.

'Could I ask you to pour us both measures?
'And please feel no need to stint.'

Syd stood as he'd been bidden, still holding the book in a loose grip by its spine.

But before he could set it back down on his chair arm, a folded newsprint cutting, almost transparent with age, fell to the floor from between its pages.

He bent to pick it up and when he saw Morgan reach out he handed it across.

'Oh!' exclaimed the old man upon unfolding it.

With an oddly muted little roar of laughter, he at once handed it back, inviting Syd to take a look.

Putting the book under one arm, Syd again did as he was asked.

The cutting was from a *Times Literary Supplement* dated sixty years earlier almost to the day. Kenneth Grahame's little riverside allegory featuring Rat, Mole, Badger and Toad was reviewed there alongside its adult peers, with the book anonymously discussed directly beneath it being *A Room with a View* by E M Forster.

'You will correct me if I am wrong,' said Morgan, 'but until the eleventh hour, was Grahame's book not scheduled to be called *The Wind in the Reeds*, possibly with a nod to a line from Shelley's *Hymn of Pan*?

'Then someone pointed out that W B Yeats had shortly beforehand published a verse collection, *The Wind Among The Reeds*. Only then did *Willows* come into Grahame's title, although willows feature barely at all in the text – far less often in fact than reeds, most particularly in your chapter seven!'

Syd re-folded the cutting, slipped it back inside the book and placed it on the chair arm, diverting his gaze from Morgan to the mantelpiece, in one of the niches of which he may or may not have noticed his retrieved, balled-up £20 note and what had to be his own rolled marijuana joint.

The likelihood is that he did spot them since he looked away again very promptly but then made no further move, as if he'd lost track of his reason for having risen.

'The sherry?' Morgan softly coaxed him.

Syd broke out of his contemplative trance and crossed the floor.

The decanter with its heavy stopper stood layered in dust. Thin cobwebs stretched across the mouths of both schooner glasses, and one contained a large dead fly.

With his back to Morgan, Syd scoured them with a finger before carefully filling them with the umber liquor, none of which he spilled in crossing the floor, passing one to Morgan then resuming his seat.

'Sir,' Syd began after both had taken sips, 'I don't quite get how you know – '

' – that this book has meaning for you?'

Schoolboy-like, Syd nodded.

Morgan smiled. 'Not too sweet for you, is it?' he asked. 'The sherry?'

Syd shook his head.

'There really is no mystery. While you slept, a college servant brought me logs – '

Syd darted a look towards the fire-irons and registered the laden basket.

'A servant younger than yourself. He appeared to find you familiar, and I enquired of him how.'

He raised a hand as if to pre-empt any plea in self-defence.

'He spoke most highly of you.'

Morgan's attention drifted over to the mantelpiece.

'He also handed in to me some items which you may have dropped from your pockets out on the landing, but we shall return to those – '

There was no doubt whatever that Syd did now steel himself not to look with Morgan directly at the note and the joint in the fireside niche.

His features seemed briefly to redden and swell.

'You would seem to be a person of some stature in your world,' Morgan went on, not unkindly. 'The world of psychedelic music?'

Nursing his sherry schooner in his lap with both hands, slowly Syd Barrett began to shake his head.

'This is a matter beyond my own competence,' said Morgan, 'but I confess that before today I had not heard of psychedelic music.

'The term "psychedelic" is itself no more than twenty years old, I understand? My friend and colleague Huxley's preferred descriptive term for the narcotics he administered to himself was "phanerothyme" – "manifest mind", which I accept is not quite so euphonic!'

He chuckled and met Syd's eye.

'You are aware perhaps of Huxley's work in this field?

His short books *The Doors of Perception* and – '

' – *Heaven and Hell*, yes I am.'

Syd was still shaking his head but in a species now of wonder as well as astonishment.

'You know Aldous Huxley?' he asked Morgan in a low hoarse voice.

'Knew, alas, knew. The poor fellow died on the same November day the American President was shot. C S Lewis too, of course.'

He raised a salt-and-pepper eyebrow. 'By the time night fell on that particular day, one was grateful to have been left standing.'

'But here is my question to you. The young man I spoke with described your music as "mind-expanding", and I have heard similar suggestions from others regarding the effects of certain narcotics on the path to enlightenment. Yet does "psychedelic" not more strictly connote bringing the mind's true nature out into the open, rather than expanding it?'

Morgan's Prospero now had more than a dash of Ariel or even Puck to him but he retained his self-awareness and on noticing he might be losing Syd he broke off and smiled down at the sherry he was making swirl in his glass.

'Put simply, it would seem that any psychedelic agent might enable us to explore our own natures, to divest ourselves of acquired assumptions, to travel to what Huxley calls "the mind's antipodes".

'So would this be a fair summary of the service psychedelic musicians seek to provide?'

*

Syd blinked.

He had leaned forward while he listened, resting his elbows on his knees and knitting his fingers together while perhaps also casting a stealthy look around the room to see if Morgan had brought in his painting while he slept.

'Sir, I don't – ' he replied, then he lapsed into a long pause before trying again.

'As I said, I don't really – '

But again words failed him, so the newly energised Morgan too sat forward.

'Do you know Thomas Traherne?' he asked.

'Does he live in Cambridge?'

'Ha, no – Oxford! Seventeenth century. He has a nice form of words for what might be said to amount to the same thing.

'He says it is to "unlearn the dirty devices of the world and become as it were a little child again".'

Morgan cocked his head to see if this sparked a response from Syd. Apart from bringing a slight furrow to his brow, it did not.

Then Morgan reached forward and although Syd moved his leg sharply aside, the older man wished only to tap his finger on *The Wind in the Willows*.

'But as your man Grahame says,' he went on, having rapped out a jaunty little tattoo, 'seeing so deep can incur penalties.

'His precise wording escapes me, but does he not suggest that there are dangers in looking with mortal eyes upon whatever is "rightly kept hidden"? I do remember that last phrase. "Rightly – "'

He nodded to himself.

'Well, there we are. Such at least was dear Grahame's opinion!'

'I do beg your pardon, sir,' said Syd, 'and it's very good of you to take an interest. But this really isn't what I've come about.

'You see, it's the painting I'm enquiring after. The music's now finished for me. I can't do anything more with that – '

Delightedly Morgan raised a finger in what looked like minor triumph.

'Because it has led you to look upon things rightly kept hidden?' he asked.

'No, I really – '

Syd then hesitated, as if to test this idea for strength.

'That is possible,' he continued less firmly. 'But I should never have been looking there in the first place. Not through music. Music was only ever meant to be a – '

He left the sentence hanging and took the remainder of his sherry in one gulp.

'I thought going into music might provide a valuable break. But it took me away. Away from where I needed to be, and I really can't talk about that now – '

'Oh but you know that you can!' Morgan replied almost before the words were out of Syd's mouth.

'You know that you must!

'I mean to say – if you cannot talk to your new comrade here, then to whom can you talk?

'Comradeship! It is our highest gift as a nation.'

A coal slipped, the fire crackled and sent a spurt of flame up the chimney.

Syd turned his head to watch it, setting down his empty schooner on the floor. Then instead of sitting back he rose to his feet, a man now apparently compromised at every turn and lost for a way to proceed.

He took a step towards the mantelpiece and a neutral observer might have imagined he was about to pocket his two bits of lost property before making himself scarce. But other forces were now at play.

He squatted before the shallow grate, and took it upon himself to pick up the poker and nudge around some of the other glowing coals, the sweet catchy smell of cut timber hanging like incense in that area of the room.

Then he took two of the short, cylindrical logs and settled them on the miniature blaze, taking some time to arrive at a final positioning – that of a largely symmetrical chevron pointing up the chimney.

He remained on his haunches, waiting to see if the logs would take but he did not stare directly into the fire. A part of his profile was turned Morgan's way, almost inviting the older man to address him again.

'You were part of a group?' Morgan duly asked. 'A pop musical group? Like those four rather refreshingly irreverent boys from Liverpool?'

'No, I – '

Syd aimed his wan smile downward, as if he'd been rumbled.

'Well yes sir, I was. For a while.'

'And people dance to your music?'

'They used to.'

Syd took a breath then slowly let it out.

'They tried to.'

He touched his gold neck chain. 'But that did become more difficult. Over time.

'Everything did.'

'So your music might be regarded more as an art form? Do you believe pop music can be a form of art?'

Syd considered this in a way that implied the question had been put to him before, possibly more than once. Finally he gave a cagey shrug.

'I think it can be. As much as sitting down is.'

Morgan, his sherry poised below his lips, fought to suppress a smile. He described a little circling motion with his glass before going on.

'Everything grew more difficult, you say? – '

Syd closed his eyes.

'It wasn't really part of the plan. The group becoming such a big commercial concern.

'I mean, we did want it – '

He gave another weary little grin.

'But then we got it. I don't suppose we realised quite how much of it was going to be about, well, punctuality.

'I know I didn't.'

'So you decided to leave the group?'

Syd made no reply.

'Or did the others leave you?'

Syd smiled a small smile and laced his fingers together again, the backs of his forearms resting lightly on his thighs.

'Were they – these others – students of art like yourself?' asked Morgan.

Syd nodded.

'Actually no,' he then said. 'Of architecture, mainly.'

He paused and his smile faded.

'Like your father, sir.'

Morgan's jaw masticated steadily. 'But I sense there was a falling out?'

Syd placed his right hand on his jacket pocket, as if to check that his pack of cigarettes was still there.

'Not as such –

'I mean, they were my friends. I grew up with some of them. There wasn't any kind of war between us. But I suppose – '

After raking back his hair from his eyes, Syd re-linked his fingers.

'I suppose it was really just a matter of being a little off-hand about things – '

'They were off-hand or you were?'

'Oh well, I'd imagine they would say it was me.'

'And would there have been any truth in that?'

Syd's clawing at his hair had only prompted one obdurate lock to spring back and spill right over his left eye. Tentatively he began to wind it around his forefinger and every last part of him – from the top of his head to the tips of his toes – seemed steeped in regret.

'I wasn't –

'I didn't think the original four of us were especially good, or even technically proficient. Well, apart from the keyboard player.

'I'm not disowning what we did. I just don't think we really knew what we wanted to do. Other than change the way that everything tended to be organised – You know, the formula?'

'Which can in itself take one some distance,' Morgan countered. 'But you have gone farther, have you not, and had substantial success? The servant referred to you as a god. Oh, the awe in that young man's face!'

Syd let go of his hair and shook his head.

'No sir. The Beatles, Bob Dylan – they're the gods. Or kings, at least. John Lennon is as far away from me as William Blake.'

His lips puckered ruefully as a memory surfaced.

'I saw it, last year – They – They were down the way from us at the studios, making *Sergeant Pepper* while we made *Piper* – '

'"Peter Piper picked a peck of pickled pepper,"' Morgan recited flawlessly under his breath.

'You're probably right,' said Syd, then his brow creased.

'Sir, it seems incredible we should be talking about me

and my work.'

'No, no!' Morgan demurred. 'No, please, do go on.'

Syd pulled a face.

'Well, my music – I suppose it did pass muster for a while.

'Then I – But then I stopped being able to reach even that level any more.'

With something of a performative flourish he swung around Morgan's way, dropping his right knee to the floor and leaning forward to prop up his chin on his raised left. Then he smiled up into Morgan's face. The same weather-reversing smile as before, the sunshine after the rain which had left his drying cheeks luminous.

In response Morgan became so self-conscious that he unnecessarily moved back both feet and shifted his sherry glass from one hand to the other.

'You see, it wasn't so much me as the time.'

Morgan looked at him confounded.

'You know, with everything happening so quickly, a year or two ago?

'It was a moment in time. People got swept up, swept along. I was commonplace really. Most of us were. As common as snowflakes.'

His smile climbed to a new level of beatitude and fresh energy seemed to flood him.

'There was one night, sir, before the group took off, when I went to the Albert Hall to hear Bob Dylan play, with my girlfriend. And when I looked around us at the audience that night, it was suddenly so obvious.

'"Look," I said to her, "it's you and me from every town."'

Morgan put his glass to his lips and, musing, left it there for a short while without sipping. It helped to steady a new tremor in his hand.

Syd straightened his back, then rose up once again to his full height.

'I really didn't deserve success,' he said.

'I just fell on my feet. But without really finding my feet, if you can see that?

'The whole time after we took off, I was just running to catch up. I mean, I enjoyed it. Some of it. But it could have been happening to anyone – '

Morgan allowed himself at last to gaze up frankly at this raggedy-haired Apollo whose extraordinary translucency was being lent a golden patina by the fire's light, and he caught his breath as if Syd were the Colossus of Rhodes made flesh. For although before that day he had never even heard of The Pink Floyd, Morgan saw – like many before him who had been magnetised by Syd's presence onstage – what this boy's former group would never have again despite all its later triumphs: one man at the heart of the spectacle.

'You must at least have looked the part,' he said in his smallest voice.

Syd's eyes widened and their wintry flash told Morgan that this too had probably not gone unsaid before – and that besides, looks could carry their own penalties.

'But the real question,' said Syd, 'the one that's brought me here, isn't why I left the group. It's why I joined up in the first place.

'Because all I ever wanted to do – ever – was paint.'

'So what is the answer?' asked Morgan. 'What sent you down this false path?'

'I don't know!

'Many reasons probably.'

Syd's smile had vanished and he tensed, suddenly looking extremely young – callow enough to be back at school, grabbed by the ear, his face being twisted up to identify the place where his cigarette smoke had earlier been absorbed into the ceiling's shadows.

'But the main one, I think, was my father.'

And for all that Syd's skin tone was already such a livid ivory-white, he then blanched.

'It was because of my father dying – '

In the echo of what he had said Syd Barrett looked as disorientated as when he first came awake in Morgan's chair.

He could just have repeated a line fed to him by a theatre prompt: a line which had not figured in his own version of the script.

As with the older man before him, his words seemed literally to have run away with him – his words or his thoughts – unless the sherry had served as a kind of truth serum.

Either way, he had now been swept into some wholly unanticipated new region.

With a curt, permission-seeking nod down at Morgan, Syd took a couple of steps past him to face the fullness of the room.

Standing between a stack of books on the floor and the low circular occasional table with its vase of crimson leaves, he looked across at the tiny budgerigar he'd been attracted to earlier, then past it.

Morgan, having levered himself sideways on a chair arm, heaved himself bodily around, then studied Syd over his shoulder before attempting to press him for more.

'Your father – ?' he began.

But still it was too soon.

With his back to Morgan, Syd absently put out a staying hand, as a parent might to warn a child that danger threatens on a road up ahead, although all he was facing was Morgan's busy assemblage of shelves, portraits and nick-nacks.

But he seemed to be staring into some vaster Narnian depths that could now, in the light of memories uncovered by what he had blurted out, be glimpsed beyond the rather loudly papered back wall.

Perhaps to assure himself that this was still nothing more than a sitting room part of the way up a college staircase, Syd turned and made for the nearer window.

*

He was so thin that he slipped easily behind the desk with its budgerigar and its photo of Morgan during his days as an Indian provincial administrator nearly half a century before.

He shouldered aside the fringe of floor-length curtain to try to see out through the glass, lowering his head and slowly leaning forward until his brow and the bridge of his nose pressed hard against the cold moist glass.

Surprisingly for the time of year the window had been left an inch or two ajar, which helped to explain at least some of the draughts in the room. But the pane just gave onto a small inner court and there were no lights at any of the facing windows.

'Until a few years ago we had such a lovely almond tree down there,' Morgan told him quietly. 'Then came substantial rebuilding. This room too was re-papered in its own rather daring way.'

A fluttery flash of red crossed Syd's line of vision.

He jerked back his head but Morgan gave a reassuring laugh.

'Ah, so that is where he has got to! I must introduce you to my earlier visitor – pretty little thing. A Red Underwing moth.'

Syd watched its progress with gimlet eyes.

'I tried to give him a snack at lunch, just to tide him over. One of my colleagues here advised me not to encourage him to leave until evening, in case a bird should get him. Hence my unlatching of that window shortly before your own arrival.'

It had come to rest again on the curtain, a small grey smudge against the burgundy red.

Without a word, and with a delicacy borne of practice as well as patience, Syd closed both his hands over it, detached it from the fabric, and transferred it to the windowsill, from which it immediately flew out through the opening and up into the night.

'Oh, bravo!' cried Morgan from his chair. 'To the elements be free!'

Syd re-latched the window.

Then he closed his eyes on the darkness, possibly trying not to think of what lay beyond this refuge which could only ever be temporary. The huge healthy elms standing motionless in the tranquil air out towards Grantchester. Those meadows where in his youth he had spent so many carefree hours. The village itself where the older thatched cottages looked no less a part of natural history than the trees which grew between them, while out beyond their lights the dark river – green as a dream and deep as death – lay silently in wait.

'I am so sorry to hear of your father,' Morgan tried again. 'Did this happen recently?'

Syd nodded.

'Seven years ago. This coming winter will be the seventh.'

He gathered himself to deliver the word. 'Cancer – '

'He must have been relatively young?'

'Not much past fifty.'

Syd broke away from the window but instead of returning to his chair he drifted on light feet over to the piano, the lid of which was pulled down. Deftly he made the fingers of one hand dance along the scratched surface of the wood like a weightless long-legged insect picking its way across a garden pond.

'Do you play?' asked Morgan.

Syd raised the lid to look at the keys then rather smartly lowered it again.

'I did start out on the piano,' he replied. 'I – '

The corner of his mouth twitched.

'My sister and I, sir – when I was seven – we won the piano prize at the Guildhall just over the road. A *Blue Danube* duet.'

He spoke as if his infant pride in the achievement were a guilty and possibly still unforgivable secret.

'But no, the true pianist was my father.'

'Like yourself he was a musician?'

Syd turned from the piano and dug his hands into the pockets of his jeans.

'He was a scientist, a pathologist. He was actually this university's Morbid Anatomist and Histologist.

'I mean, that was his work. But he did play the piano, very well, and he sang. He was an exceptional artist too. He made drawings of funghi, for his own books –

'He – '

Abruptly Syd reined himself in.

'A man of many parts, then?' said Morgan into the deepening silence.

'But yes,' Syd finally resumed. 'My father was – Well, he did value music very highly. And I think that may have been why – '

'Why what, my dear fellow?'

Syd seemed to shrink a little where he stood.

Briefly he puffed out his cheeks and looked over to his left, his eyes alighting on a table which supported something, possibly a primitive musical instrument, which he may not have noticed before.

He stepped across to look at it more closely: a smooth white box with wires attached to its base, like an outsized Jew's harp.

Morgan startled him with an explosive little laugh.

'Oh!' he called over, 'I should be most surprised if any member of your musical family could get a tune out of that!'

With his hands still tucked into his hip pockets, Syd ducked his head to investigate the strings.

'Is this telephone wire?' he asked.

'It is! Gifted to me on a British Association tour of Africa. The people in Uganda would play such things as they worked on the roads.'

Syd paced around it, tilting his head with genuine fascination, not simply to prevaricate.

'Please now,' he heard Morgan then say, as if from a greater distance, 'do come back here, and I will continue to do what I can to help with your enquiry.'

Syd looked up to find Morgan had turned again to face his hearth.

Sunk deep in his chair, he'd canted himself sideways to the right, and like a passenger on a train awaiting the arrival of the ticket inspector he was holding up his emptied sherry glass by the side of his head.

As Syd approached, the nape of Morgan's neck showed itself barely to have aged at all, and the hair directly above it was almost as dark as it would have been during the reign of Queen Victoria.

'There can't be much sherry left in the decanter,' Morgan said when Syd came back into view and he passed up his glass. 'I suggest we polish it off.'

After Syd did the honours Morgan patted the vacant chair, bringing up some specks of dust. He seemed to have dragged it an inch or two closer to his own.

Again Syd looked as if he needed to take off his feet what little weight he carried.

He let the chair receive him, threw Morgan a glance, then gazed into the fire.

Morgan looked at him closely, as if making a series of actual, medical checks. His attentiveness to the younger man was so disarming that if Syd had not stood so irrefutably in need of it, he might have felt unnerved.

Morgan's fastidiousness with language too could have been forbidding. Yet for all the continuing sharpness of his mind, there was still more than a little of Thomas Traherne's winning childlike innocence about him, and his small voice, never louder than *mezzo piano*, held such a welcome, as did his pouchy smile. This untidy literary lion was a welcoming committee of one, and in the face of such relentless cordiality it would have been hard for any man, whatever his quandary, to keep up his natural mid-twentieth-century English reserve.

So they sat: the Grand Old Man of English Letters beside London's Face of the Summer of Love, two sons of Albion at the closing-in of an autumn evening. A moment had undeniably arrived.

Syd let his head loll back against the chair's high wing.

Then he rested the palm of his hand on the small, green-bound book which in size was so similar to the logs in the wicker basket. With his eyes trained upon the ceiling, or on whoever might be looking down from rarer heights, he could have been about to give sworn evidence in a courtroom.

'You were close to your father?' asked Morgan.

His hand still resting on *The Wind in the Willows*, Syd shook his head.

'It's quite a big family, sir. I have two older brothers, an older and a younger sister –

'The house was busy, Dad was busy. I used – I used to like to make him laugh. He never used to mind being disturbed by some joke or other.'

He started to shrug then stopped himself.

'But he was – He was always kind, always encouraging – '

He turned his eyes on Morgan with a look of such desolation.

'I wish I'd known him longer.'

'You would have been precisely how old at his death?'

'Fifteen. Very nearly sixteen.

'He – He was in a lot of pain near the end. In the nights we all heard him crying out. It went through the house – '

He gave a firm nod.

'But I wish I'd known him longer. Known him better. I'd assumed there would be time. I just –

'I wasn't really ready for him to be gone. Not for good – '

Morgan produced a hitherto unseen handkerchief and gave his nose a loud and thorough blow that may have been in part strategic.

Syd smiled inwardly.

'This is absurd of me, I know,' he said. 'To be talking like this. About what I've lost.'

'What makes you say that?'

'Well, even just in relation to yourself, sir. I mean, from what you say, you've never really known a father at all.'

Morgan took some sherry, possibly noting that however dislocated Syd might at times have seemed, he'd been paying some attention too.

'One cannot miss what one never knew,' he replied, dusting at his jacket cuff. 'And there is no good time to be deprived of a parent.

'Dodgson – Lewis Carroll – lost his father when he was thirty-six and he claimed it was the greatest blow that fell on his life. Albert Einstein too described his loss as the deepest shock he ever experienced.'

He put a hand to the left side of his moustache and encouraged it.

'In retrospect, although my feelings were perhaps not so closely involved, losing my father can be seen as the defining moment of my own life – since the world I was then brought up in lacked a significant male figure.'

He gave another of his infectiously thin little explosions of laughter which sounded not far short of a sneeze.

'In the event, it was a close run thing for me. As a small fatherless Victorian child, my widowed mother and maiden aunts did insist on growing my hair and putting me in dresses!

'Once, when a coachman mistook me for a girl, I was told to go back and explain to him that I was in fact a little boy. Do you know what the man said?'

Syd looked up from his lap into Morgan's suddenly bulbous eyes.

'He said to me, steady as you like, "Yes, miss"!'

To keep a straight face Syd bit on his lip.

'Getting down to the brassiest of brass tacks, however,' Morgan immediately continued, 'I suspect that when, nearly seven years ago, your own childhood entered upon the branching paths of youth, there may have been especial difficulties – ?'

Syd tilted up his chin.

'You perhaps imagine that had your father lived,' Morgan elaborated, 'these seven years may have taken a different course?

'Slap me down if I speak out of turn but have you missed your father's supervision? Is it possible that, without it, you have been given too much freedom?'

Syd glanced his way, and with a dizzying level of subtlety Morgan allowed Syd to see him glance in turn, for a fraction of a second, at the joint in the mantelpiece niche; then in a tone and with an expression which communicated that he was in fact talking of far more robust potential challenges, he said:

'Those agents of psychedelia which we earlier discussed? The doors of perception and so forth – ?'

Syd could be in no doubt what he meant and he had no glib answer.

'When you first arrived here,' Morgan pressed him, 'you rather appeared – '

'I know how I can appear,' Syd told the fire with a nod. 'And it can sometimes be – convenient,' he added. 'To appear that way.'

He chewed his lip.

'Not always, but sometimes.

'It's true too that occasionally I don't face things properly.

'I get – Oh, I get frustrated. I always have. There are times I behave poorly. To girls, especially to girls – And times too when I'm genuinely quite – unwell.'

He took a deep breath. 'And I'm sorry, but that's all a different thing.'

Morgan showed him a deferring palm.

'What I also meant,' Morgan explained, 'was the freedom to follow your heart?'

Syd came back at that like lightning.

'My heart isn't really what I think I've followed.'

The resolution in his voice seemed to arrest Syd himself as much as Morgan.

'Again I must ask: how so?'

Syd screwed up his face as if he'd just been told he had only four months to live, or else been condemned to live out a further four decades.

'Absurd. I know this is absurd – '

'It was the music,' said Syd, his face still clenched.

'Before Dad died, I never meant –

'When I was younger, it was just a diversion. Playing music, performing.'

'A diversion from your art?' Morgan sought to clarify.

'From drawing, from painting. I was always going to follow art. Only that.'

'But in your sorrow you tried to lose yourself in music. As a way to escape?'

Syd opened his eyes then blinked them slowly, straight at Morgan.

'There are all manner of ways to escape, sir.

'But no, not lose myself. I rather – Well, I rather tried to find my father again. Through music.'

He scoured his tongue around his lower inner jaw.

'I told you this was absurd. But that was just how I thought we might – I wondered whether, in that way, we might reconnect. Whether music could be a kind of doorway to my Dad.

'And, for a time, it seemed it might be. Then it was just – Then it became too late.'

He tipped the entire second glass of sherry down his throat, juddering the glass's rim against his upper teeth.

'It was never going to last,' he said then. 'The music.

'I suppose I always knew that really.

'Whatever new things I want to give people – you know, musically – they don't seem to want them any more. It's finished.

'I've queered my own pitch.'

*

Morgan drew off his glasses, folding them shut in one hand then holding them in his clenched fist up by his temple.

'The arts,' he reflected, 'could be seen to be our chief means of communication with the dead. And we each respond in our own ways to the loss of those we love.

'I well remember the depth of my gloom when I attained the age of my father at his death. I was completing *Howards End* and despite all the expectations of those around me, already I wondered if I should ever be able to match it. Something in me, too, seemed to reach a stopping point.'

Syd gave a doleful smile. 'But I've never come up with anything like *Howards End*, sir! It's not as if I've got a body of work I can no longer live up to. I hardly even got started. From a very early stage, it was just producing to order.'

Morgan waved his folded glasses as if to say that he registered this but wanted to file it away for the moment.

'You are producing new music, though? Outside of your group? You say people don't seem to want it – '

'I don't know that I want it myself.

'I – I've been trying – trying and failing – to put some verse of Joyce's to music.'

'James Joyce?'

Syd nodded. 'That and some other things.

'But to want more time away from it now – another break – it makes me feel like a fraud. To consider any form of art as if it were paid work, from which one wants time off –

'I mean, you'd never find John Lennon wanting to give up music just to stay at home and put his feet up.'

'Is that what you want to do?

'And where is your home, as a point of interest? Do you still have one in Cambridge?'

'Well, my mother still lives in Hills Road,' Syd answered absently.

'With its many privet hedges,' said Morgan with a bow.

'But I'm – You could say I'm nowhere, now.'

Quickly he corrected that.

'No, London. That's where I'm supposed to be working. I rent a place in central London. It's not – It isn't especially suitable.'

'But it's not the music's fault,' he said, returning to his main theme.

'Not the music itself. It's all the business around it that I find so – All the middlemen – The need to keep churning out new things, whether one feels driven to or not.

'I very much used to enjoy playing older things, other people's music, the way we did at the beginning – '

'People such as?'

'Oh, I doubt you'll have come across them, sir. Black American blues players mainly. "Race music" they call it over there – '

He made an impatient face.

'I really can't imagine any of this interests you.

'The bigger point is that I've never really stuck at anything. I thought I would stick at art – at Camberwell. But now –

'Well, now I've kind of missed the bus.'

'Which bus would this be?'

'I didn't stay long enough with art. I made a start but I

didn't find my direction, my own visual language. I didn't – Any gift that I had, I didn't honour it.'

Not without some awkwardness Morgan resettled his glasses on his nose one-handed.

'And were you gifted? As an artist?'

Syd paused.

'I may have been shown to be, perhaps. One day.'

'So now, in coming here, you are seeking to turn back the clock, in order to undo all that you say has gone wrong for you since effectively you renounced fine art?'

Syd's hand was back at his throat, agitating his rosary of a neck chain.

'Everything that's backfired, yes,' he agreed.

'And by way of the symbolic act of retrieving a painting which you believe should never have been exchanged for filthy lucre, the genie can be returned to the bottle?'

Syd turned to Morgan as if for the first time, to those ample yet elusive features which seemed to offer either too much or too little for the eye to work with, and which made trying to pin them down now like trying to remember how one tune went while listening to another.

'And what will happen if this does not prove to be the outcome?' Morgan asked in his mild, ever-curious manner.

Syd didn't answer so Morgan re-phrased his question.

'What if the genie prefers to stay out in the open air?'

Syd gripped the arm of his chair.

'Oh,' he said with a new, opaque grin, 'then the game really would be up!'

And with a nod first at Kenneth Grahame's book, inside

which sat the cutting preserving the unsigned review written in fact by Virginia Woolf, then at the window beyond which the city's river coursed along the backs of so many of the colleges – and with a look, it had to be said, as if he had just arrived at the antipodes of his own mind – Syd Barrett gave a ripe, dog-fox yap of a laugh and he said to Morgan Forster:

'Well, that would be it, wouldn't it? The outer darkness.

'I mean, what else would there be?

'I'd have to load my pockets with stones and jump in the Cam.'

Morgan clapped a hand to his cheek.

'Oh!' he exclaimed, 'That dirty little prettified river! To think that it could kill!'

They both laughed then, looking square into each other's eyes.

'It is probably wise not to joke about such things,' said Morgan.

Syd's smile wavered but he made it stay in place.

Morgan finished his sherry and set it down beside him where earlier the teacup had been.

'You seem to shy away from obligatory creation for your public,' Morgan continued. 'But could you not paint and draw simply to meet your own needs?'

'That's all I've ever done,' Syd replied at once.

'I've never painted or drawn for anyone else. Even when – Even as a boy I wouldn't take commissions. You know, from family and friends? I've never – Well, I've never had any measurable commercial prospects. Not in that field.'

A log shifted on the fire, the space it left sending out new mellow light and warmth. With the window closed, the room was already a good deal cosier.

'And besides, sir, somehow I have to make a living first. Get somewhere more suitable to live.'

'But you have a home in Hills Road?'

'My mother does.'

'I lived with my own mother until I was past retirement age.'

This seemed to puzzle Syd.

'You haven't always been here? I thought – '

'It only seems I have been here since the dawn of time! Though I should imagine I have been here for the entirety of your own life. When were you born?'

'January the sixth 1946,' Syd told him, offering up his answer like a child far from home remembering his address for a policeman.

'There you have it! Exactly the year of my coming here, or my coming back. I took my undergraduate degree at King's, d'you see, at the turn of the century.'

He slid his glasses off again and as if to counteract a new wave of tiredness he kneaded his eyeballs robustly with thumb and first finger.

'It doesn't do to stay around a place like Cambridge one's whole life. It is, I think, for the very old or the very young.'

He threw Syd what may have been intended as a pointed look but his fogged-up eyes seemed to see nothing and in that moment, by the new light from the fire, he looked terribly fragile.

'In the middle years,' he made himself go on, 'one should go away, gain experience –

'Which is indeed what you have done, or rather what you are doing. There is still plenty of time for you to come back later, perhaps even to your mother's home. You would then be able to enjoy all the art of the Fitzwilliam Museum virtually on your doorstep, and the collections at Kettle's Yard – you know of these?'

Syd nodded, and Morgan bowed back.

'There are worse arrangements that a man might make than to stay with his mother. An unconventional man, that is. But who would really wish to be other? Three hundred years ago, did Newton not withdraw to his mother's home and develop the laws of gravity!'

His voice was sounding thinner and even after replacing his glasses he seemed to be having difficulty both in keeping Syd in his sights and in supporting his great head's weight.

'January the sixth – ' he could be heard murmuring as if to some small unseen pet sitting curled in his lap. 'January the sixth – '

Syd leaned in closer with a faintly perturbed frown.

But Morgan then smiled to himself. 'That would make you exactly sixty-seven years and five days younger than I!'

Syd made his own calculation.

'You were born on New Year's Day, sir?'

'In 1879. A mere two decades after Darwin made his case that our existence might be explained without invoking a divine creator – '

His eyes seemed to pop at what could have been another rogue statement passing his lips almost before he'd been conscious of having formed the thought, but the bleariness hadn't left them, and though his words were still clear his line of argument seemed to have stalled.

'I came out of the nineteenth century,' he resumed, as if consciously marking time. 'We belong to different epochs, you and I. But the alignments of the stars would have been the same.'

He pointed a finger heavenward.

'I was told your music is "spaced out". You are up with all this celestial business, are you? Astronomy? More particularly, astrology?'

The younger man who had led his group on so many headlong charges through *Interstellar Overdrive* and *Astronomy Domine* half-shook his head.

'It is not my own strongest suit,' Morgan went on, seeming to rediscover a touch of his earlier vigour on warming to this subject.

'For instance, I should be hard-pressed to explain quite why our present period is being termed the Age of Aquarius. We both, of course, were born under the zodiac's previous sign, Capricorn the sea-goat – '

Again Syd shook his head, his expression betraying a fear that the old gentleman's mind really might now at last have begun to wander.

'But there we are,' Morgan said, as if impatient to move on. 'Our January births make us two of a kind! The old goat and the new – '

His weighty head swayed on his neck as he smiled across at Syd.

'Your plight, though, makes me anxious,' he said with sudden solemnity. 'Your mother must be anxious too? Is she aware of how things stand?'

Syd gave a non-committal nod.

'It is bitter enough to lose a father,' said Morgan. 'How much more bitter to lose a son – a deprivation of which I have had some experience, albeit at a remove.'

He gestured at the book still balancing on Syd's chair arm.

'And poor, poor Grahame in this respect.

'You will be familiar with his travails?'

Syd swallowed but made no reply.

He may not have known what Morgan meant. Or, given his own straits, Syd may have preferred not to dwell on what the older man had to be getting at: the recovery from railway tracks on Oxford's Port Meadow of the corpse of Grahame's undergraduate son, the child to whom he had first told his *Willows* tales at bedtime; and this just a year before the surrogate son on whom J M Barrie had modelled his Peter Pan possibly gave up his life too while swimming to the south of the same city. Certain footsteps are harder than others to follow in.

Morgan shifted around, as if to make a remark to someone else in the room, then he murmured a few indistinct words.

'What was that, sir?' Syd asked.

'Oh! Did I speak? Some lines of Eliot, from the *Four Quartets*. I sit here, d'you see, and read old Eliot aloud. I no longer have passages by heart as once I did, but the one I am thinking of relates to music.

'It posits that some music is heard so deeply that it ceases to be music at all. One rather is the music, for as long as the music lasts.'

'As long as it lasts,' said Syd quietly. 'Yes.'

'To a verbalist like me music does seem the deepest of the arts,' Morgan declared. 'Only through music does one get near to the centre of reality – '

Then he cleared his throat at length, seeming manfully to be trying to take himself in hand.

'I say – ' he began.

He reached down, without looking, for his empty sherry glass but missed it by some distance. He swung his arm and missed it again.

'I say now,' he repeated, 'would you mind awfully putting a little drop of drinking water into my glass, which I do not quite seem to be able to – '

Syd came forward in a crouch from his chair, scooped up the glass for Morgan then stood beside him, looking around for either a tap or jug.

'You may use some of the boiled water from the kettle,' Morgan told him, indicating the electric model near the coal scuttle.

'It will have cooled down completely since I made my last cup of tea.'

Syd wasted no time in doing as he'd been asked.

Morgan was a little gaspy in reaching for the filled glass, which he drained in one gulp then held up for a refill.

'If you would be so good,' he panted, moistening his lips with tiny darts of his tongue, a gleam of mounting helplessness in his eyes.

'I am – sorry to put you to this bother. One can easily become, at this age, a little – dry.'

After swallowing his second glassful Morgan seemed to grow steadier. But rather as Syd had earlier, he put up a staying hand so that he could fully gather himself before he felt equipped to continue.

Syd resumed his seat and waited, closing his fingers around the cigarette pack in his pocket but not taking it out, eyeing the two items in the mantelpiece niche.

'I am uncertain,' Morgan said finally, both hands now clasped beside his left cheek, 'what point we had reached in our deliberations.'

Syd sat forward, making as if to answer but Morgan simply went on:

'What I would like to ask is why, at this stage in your life, you regard the stakes as so very high.'

Syd looked back at him, trying to fathom if this was a further rhetorical question.

'I believe the phrase today is "make-or-break"?' Morgan prompted.

'Well, I – ' Syd began, and immediately he floundered.

'I mean to say,' Morgan put to him, 'to all intents and purposes you are still a free agent. And having started out with what one might term certain advantages, like many in your generation you may continue to do with your life virtually as you please.

'From my own vantage point – if you will forgive me – I

cannot see why you should not be riding on magical cushions of air, the prince of all you survey!'

He paused.

'But would I be correct in thinking that you define yourself by what you create?'

'Is that what you do?' Syd surprised him by asking back.

'I?'

'I mean, you probably do now,' said Syd, 'having been creative for so very long.'

On hearing that, Morgan threw him a startled look.

'But did you at the beginning, sir? Did you want to be a writer from boyhood?'

Morgan tented his hands above his eyes as if to concentrate his thoughts. This made the set of his features hard to read, so Syd may not have been expecting the gleeful note in his voice when finally he replied.

'D'you know,' he said, 'I am told that at the age of six my ambitions lay in quite a different direction. "I should like to be a flower," I am supposed to have said. "A primrose that nobody picks"!'

'That doesn't sound so bad,' said Syd after thinking it over. 'But no, I wouldn't say I define myself. Not consciously – '

'Then is it that you feel driven to make your mark upon the world? Is this why you feel that otherwise there may be no point in going on?'

'No I don't – ' said Syd. 'No that's not necessarily what motivates me. I don't think it ever has been.

'It's more – Well, I think I'd like to make my case, rather than my mark.'

Morgan nodded. 'Yet from what I am led to believe – by our young friend who delivered the logs – already you have entered the hall of fame.'

Syd sat even further forward, perched now at the seat's very edge.

'I think –

'What I've always thought is that I have to create. For myself. It doesn't terribly matter whether anyone else responds to it.'

He reconsidered what he'd said.

'Obviously, it's nice if people get what you're trying to do – '

'And they have indeed "got" your music,' Morgan suggested.

'Not always.'

Syd sniffed and narrowed his eyes.

'Outside London we often had cans and bottles thrown at us.

'Some people in Dunstable once poured beer over us on stage from the balcony.'

'Ah,' said Morgan. 'There never is any accounting for Dunstable.'

'Honestly sir, others have described the creative act far better than I can. You maybe have yourself. But to me it's never been optional – making art, making music. Making sense of everything that's otherwise, well, that's otherwise just too much. But – '

'Everything?'

'Oh, you know – the world? Life?'

'Indeed I do,' said Morgan. 'The muddle.'

'But what seems to have happened is that I've stopped being able to do it. Any of it. I don't know how on earth I ever managed it in the first place.

'And because it's gone, it's as if I'm going too. Out of the world.

'Kind of dying off in instalments.'

Morgan looked across at Syd above his spectacle rims, much of the skittishness of minutes earlier gone from his eyes and around his lips.

He lugged himself forward and seemed on the point of standing, then thought better of it and sat back again, seemingly a little dizzied.

'As it falls out, I did once have something to say about the act of creation,' he told Syd. 'Had I the confidence of my legs at this moment, I would go and look out the essay and give it you to read.

'It is not a particularly long passage, nor a particularly brilliant one, but it does have some relevance to your point about how "on earth" these things seem to get done.

'If you will allow me, I shall try to paraphrase.'

He closed his eyes and steepled his fingers.

'I was trying to make sense of the act of creation in any field – so this may apply to your music as much as to any other form, although far be it from me to teach you the mysteries of your own profession.

'But I suggested that when man creates, he is taken out of himself. Put another way, he lets down a bucket into his subconscious, so to speak, and draws up something that is normally beyond his reach. He then mixes this thing with his normal experiences, and out of the mixture he makes a work of art.'

'Well, yes,' said Syd, 'that does sound – '

Morgan raised a finger to show he hadn't finished.

'Now this creative process may well be aided by knowledge of the world, and by ingenuity when it comes to technique. But it cannot exist without the stuff from the bucket. And this subconscious stuff does not simply jump into one's bucket whenever one might ask it to.'

Syd hesitated before saying, 'I think you make a very good case, sir.'

'But do you see my specific point? That once the work is complete, the creator – as you yourself put it to me – will look back and wonder how on earth he did it?'

He paused, for just long enough to ease off his glasses.

'And of course he cannot possibly find an answer, because he did not in fact do it "on earth"!'

Syd was already nodding, a faraway look in his eyes.

'One might refer here to Milton's claim that *Paradise Lost* came to him in the form of nightly dictation from a celestial muse.'

Morgan paused as if in his mind this awesome seventeenth-century bedside scene were being reconstructed specifically for him.

'But I go on, in my essay, to give the example of Coleridge's famous dream, assisted by opium – you know it? – during which the poet delved deep into his subconscious to find

Kubla Khan. But when he woke, and started to write the poem up, he was interrupted by a man who came to call on business – '

'The person from Porlock,' said Syd, now also with a faraway sound in his voice.

'Quite so.'

Morgan refitted his glasses, then using both hands he made an elegant evaporating gesture.

'And that put an end to Coleridge's connection with the subconscious.

'You see, he had created but he didn't know how.

'The poem belonged to another world!'

'Of course,' he went on, 'I may be barking up quite the wrong tree in seeing things this way. And "stuff not simply jumping into the bucket" could be dismissed as the most egregious excuse for simply failing to produce art. Especially coming from a man who has spent the better part of his life in creative idleness!'

Syd looked up blankly from the fire at him.

'Oh!' Morgan scoffed. 'You are not aware that my fifth and final novel was published as long ago as 1924? The year that St Petersburg was renamed Leningrad and the *Ziegfeld Follies* opened on Broadway? Our women were still wearing shingled hair!'

When Syd still said nothing, Morgan laughed.

'You do seem to be labouring under various misapprehensions! That I have a son with whom I eat sandwiches, for example. That I have always lived in King's.

'Do you actually know anything about me? Not that there is any reason why you should – although you have rather sought me out here.'

Chastened, Syd lowered his eyes and studied his hands.

'I should not be at all surprised if you have never read a word I've written!' cried Morgan, sounding tickled pink by the idea.

Syd raised his head with great deliberation but before he could make what seemed likely to be a most embarrassing admission, Morgan diverted him.

'To return to you: are you absolutely sure you wish to finish with music? Having already covered so much ground to get to where you are?'

In quiet despair Syd touched a finger to his eyebrow.

'Some days I am sure, yes. Some weeks, even. But –

'What I really like to do is experiment. Try to make an entirely new kind of music. In the group, oh –

'In the group I got so tired of our sound palette. I wanted to bring in female singers, maybe a saxophonist –

'But in those circumstances – contractual demands, and having to make new records to capitalise on the sales of older ones, and to reproduce those records on stage on a routine basis – Well, there's little chance to do anything very different. One is kind of – locked in.'

'It sounds to me as if you became bored.'

Syd gave a nod of earnest agreement. 'And I think that's not at all uncommon,' he replied, 'in the music world.

'You have to be a type of person, or type of artist, to be able to marshal yourself to meet those demands. And even if you succeed in all that, the shine gets rubbed off what you produce.'

He cleared his throat.

'Though none of what I produced would have had much appeal for you, sir – '

Morgan shook his head vehemently.

'That very much misses the point. My own tastes are neither here nor there.'

He jerked back his thumb at the Picasso print.

'Many people of my generation and younger find nothing appealing in the work of this reprobate. The more discerning among them would hold that his work still needs doing.'

Syd too was shaking his head, though not in protest. 'But producing music, or any art, in the way I described – it's just a different sort of a conversation from the one I thought I was getting into.'

He paused.

'And in many ways, going solo this year has been worse than being in the group.'

'You wish you'd stayed?'

Syd smiled and touched his neck chain.

'No, by the end I don't think they'd have had me, sir.

'You asked just now about me finishing with music. I think it's more that music finished with me.

'It's gone. I'm an utterly busted flush.'

At that, Syd rocked himself back up onto his feet and took a long sideways step towards the door.

Even while he seemed to be fully engaging with Morgan

he was still manifestly just hovering, waiting to cut his losses and march out.

'But it can't last, can it?' he snorted, his mood having flipped.

He stood clenching and unclenching his fists, showing Morgan just how menacing he may have seemed to his intimates – not only in a self-destructive way – when all his frustrations could no longer be contained.

'What we do in our groups and on our own, it's not meant to last!'

A brand new brittleness was abroad in the room. Syd even moved as if the ice underfoot had thinned further while he'd been sitting, but although he sounded incensed he looked plain lost.

'We can't keep singing indefinitely that we hope we die before we get old! But what are we going to do instead?'

'Is that what you sing?'

Morgan was working his way to the front of his chair. Peering up timidly from behind his spectacles he seemed more mole-like than ever.

Syd shrugged.

'So little of it is actually about the music. It's more what we seem to stand for. People soon stop listening and they see you as – well, as a type of messiah. They want you to die for them, without dying.'

He gave another rasping laugh.

'Once we've run dry, they might prefer it if we did cease to exist. Or even – '

'Or even?'

'Perhaps there are people out there who might decide to – you know – take the matter into their own hands. If in the end we disappoint or offend them.

'In New York this summer there's already been something ugly. It happened to an artist. A very good modern artist. Not a musician, though he's been closely involved with a music group –

'Somebody shot at him, they tried to assassinate him.

'Things can get out of hand. One starts to wonder who might be next.'

Both men stiffened.

It could have been a blast from upstairs again as the transistor was re-tuned. Or perhaps the sudden loud burst of a manly hymn had carried all the way across the college's front court from the Chapel. But it was impossible for either Morgan or Syd not to notice it, Syd standing half way between his chair and the door, Morgan beginning to struggle to his feet as if in a bid to bring him back.

'You concern me, young man,' Morgan called over, seriously short of breath, as the chorus of voices faded and he levered himself up into a standing position.

'All this talk of death – '

Syd's slow blink seemed to tell Morgan not to take what he said too literally.

'Bertrand Russell once suggested something to me,' Morgan forged on nonetheless, not looking as four-square as he might, and panting now quite hard.

'What Russell pointed out – '

Rocking where he stood, he closed his eyes and had to pause to get his breathing back under control, then the words came in a rush:

'What he told me was that people will say laughingly exactly what they mean, hoping thus to conceal it.'

His shoulders seemed to crowd in on each other.

He reached out towards Syd, and made another in his wide repertoire of sketched-out yet expressive little gestures – a courteous, almost regal turning motion of the hand.

But then for no immediately apparent reason he tried to manoeuvre himself around towards the hearth.

He staggered. His legs began to buckle.

Finding it impossible to stay upright, he had been intending to drop back down into his chair but he had turned the wrong way. And now, unlike the time before while Syd was still asleep, he was unable to rediscover his balance.

To Syd's self-evident horror he was about to topple into the fire.

The younger man sprang towards him.

Both cried out as Syd grabbed Morgan's elbow, wheeling him away from the fire but almost losing his own footing as their combined centre of gravity shifted.

For two very long moments they reeled in a chaotic little tango between the armchairs, Syd clinging bodily to Morgan's dead weight like the angel wrestling Jacob in Epstein's monumental alabaster carving.

Morgan's bulk may have looked feathery but in fact he had great substance. Another, louder, cry escaped Syd as he fought to stabilise the pair of them.

They seemed to bounce off the chair Morgan had been using, then collided straight into Syd's so that it slewed around, away from the hearth. This at least served to stop them spinning on.

Syd dug his Cuban heels into the floorboards as an extra brake, although following a throttled exclamation of what may have been "Hold on to your hats!" Morgan became entirely lifeless in his grip.

'Sir – ' Syd managed to gasp in fresh alarm.

The old author's face slid lower down the front of Syd's buttoned jacket. Then his massy tweed form became so limp that Syd's hold on him began inexorably to loosen.

There was no way to keep the great British humanist upright.

But Syd managed at least to swerve him towards his own former chair and when the backs of Morgan's knees met the edge of its seat he crumpled down into its slightly more forgiving upholstery and not directly on to the floor.

Syd however, starting to overbalance and unable to extricate his arms in time, crumpled with him.

As Morgan's upper torso slapped against the cushioning, Syd did not quite fall forward on top of him. At the very last he twisted himself fractionally to one side. He dropped to his knees hard by the chair but his left arm stayed coiled around Morgan's waist, and now it was pinned beneath him.

Pinned tight.

Unlike his chin, which he was able to lift away from its lodge on the seat cushion next to Morgan's right thigh, Syd's arm right up to the shoulder was so firmly wedged in behind his slumped host that there was no way of releasing it except by using his free hand to lever Morgan's upper body forward.

Yet when Syd darted a look up at Morgan's inert face – mouth open, eyes closed, crooked glasses pushed up close to receding hairline – he must have wondered if he dared to disturb him, for fear of adding new complications to whatever internal malfunction had just shut him down.

And for the second time since his arrival, it may even have crossed Syd's mind that this pale, untwitching face might not belong to someone who was still living.

*

All this talk of death – Those had been Morgan's words of remonstration so shortly before things took this calamitous turn.

Contorted on the floor, the fire's warmth on his back, Syd closed his eyes on the dark room's bedeckings.

He bowed his head inside Morgan's fug of mothballs and ripening fabric, sherry fumes, shaving soap and perhaps a whiff of hair pomade, and he seemed physically to deflate as he let out a sigh even bleaker than the one he'd given on finishing his first cigarette, when still he had imagined he was on his own in the room.

'Oh – '

On reopening his eyes, he reached for Morgan's left wrist to feel for a pulse.

Both the old man's hands lay stiff and upturned in his lap. But as soon as Syd's fingers made contact with his papery flesh, he made to flick them away.

As if burned, Syd withdrew his hand and stuffed it into his mess of black hair. At the same time he tried, quite in vain, to work free the arm that was trapped at the small of Morgan's back.

'Sir, I – ' he began.

'If – ' Morgan interjected, lifting his hand a short distance but otherwise staying marmoreally still.

'If you would give me just a moment or two longer to re-compose myself, I should be most grateful.'

Already he sounded more composed than Syd had any right to expect.

But his voice was at odds with his continuing stillness. It seemed to be coming from somewhere remote, as if he had not only let down a bucket into his subconscious then left it there, but had loaded all the rest of himself into it first.

Grasping the chair's arm, Syd looked up and found his eyes remained closed but his lower jaw no longer hung loose and there now seemed to be, if anything, an amused set to his lips.

'I do apologise for this,' Morgan murmured, his raised hand still aloft.

'No, no,' Syd said just as softly. 'It's I who should apologise. For vexing you like this, for overtaxing you – '

Morgan let the back of his hand drop down briefly onto Syd's.

'Please, I am far from vexed! But I do become so easily ironed out.

'I suspect indigestion rather than heart lay at the root of what just happened. You may be able to smell food on my breath? – '

Syd swung himself up on to both knees.

'Should somebody be fetched, sir?' he asked, glancing around the room. 'You don't have a phone in here, do you?'

Morgan almost smiled.

'I make what calls I must from the porter's lodge. But no – Thank you, there is no need for that. One might simply say – '

He frowned, as if the impact of some earlier, less specific blow had only just been felt. Then he smiled.

'One might say that at this late stage I sometimes annex more than I can govern.'

His smile spread, and he reached up to reposition his glasses.

'That I carry home from the shops more than I can unpack!'

Taking hold of his chair's arms, he braced himself then arced his back just sufficiently for Syd to pull his own arm clear.

'But I can hardly complain,' he went on as he resettled, turning his head to beam his cordial smile down at Syd. 'After all, I am just a tiny night-light, suffocated in its own wax, and on the point of expiring!'

Syd looked up into his eyes and behind his glasses they were not just dancing, they glistened too with a film of tears.

When he saw that Syd had noticed, Morgan again made a bustle of bringing out his handkerchief and gave his nose a second comprehensive blow during which he may have managed to slip a blotting corner beneath each of his spectacle lenses.

'Now look here,' he said, newly businesslike, when he had finished.

'To return to your own much more urgent matter: how are we to keep you clear of the River Cam?'

But it wasn't so easy for Syd to draw a line under the episode.

He seemed winded, unable to get back on his feet. He sank into a sitting position on the floor by Morgan's chair, hands clapped over his raised knees, looking out at the room from this new perspective.

'As a very much younger man,' Morgan went on regardless, 'in fact at much the age you are now, I once found myself similarly dallying with thoughts of giving the whole thing up as a bad job. But I wrote down two reasons that sprang to mind for actually persevering.

'Leaving aside the first of them, the second was a reminder of how ceaselessly beautiful nature could be.'

He gestured at the Kenneth Grahame volume which had been knocked to the floor when the two men careered together into the other chair and now sat unopened just ahead of them, ten or twelve inches from Morgan's undisturbed sherry schooner.

'And for you, as someone who has quoted directly from this book and also showed such a sure touch with my visiting moth, I would suggest the delights of nature may be similarly significant?'

Slowly Syd shook his head, his face remaining closed.

'I do think I should go, sir,' he said. 'This isn't doing you any good.'

Morgan let out a genteel cackle.

'Oh!' he replied. 'You refer to my physical well-being? With respect, that is something for me rather than you to decide!

'For more years than I can remember my health has been failing, as is only to be expected. I will not regale you with the list of my debilities, but you may take it that I am not an unfamiliar figure at Addenbrooke's Hospital – '

He broke off as a thought occurred.

' – where your father must also have been well-known, I imagine. On the other side of the stethoscope, as it were?'

'Yes sir,' Syd quietly agreed after a moment's pause.

He reached into his jacket pocket and this time produced

his cigarette pack.

'You really don't mind if I stay a short while longer?'

Morgan struck the arm of his chair approvingly.

'I insist on it!'

'What will not be apparent to you is that, apart from my small lapse just now, in your company I have found myself oddly rejuvenated,' Morgan continued.

'In the year of your exhibition, d'you see, I suffered my first mild stroke, from which I made a recovery, although not quite a full one. Since then I am aware that my articulacy, like my memory, has not always been of the clearest. I do not as a matter of fact generally say very much at all nowadays. No Cambridge donkey need fear for its hind legs here! People often therefore assume I hear virtually nothing as well.'

He gave his little hoot.

'Although – as you mentioned regarding the effect that modifiers of consciousness are perceived to have had upon yourself – it can at times be "convenient" to appear incommunicable.

'Sometimes my visitors – Oh, hearses are hilarious by comparison!

'In speaking with you, however, I seem to have been granted a remission from my many and varied ailments. It is like having been given a fresh coat of paint, though I fear it will vanish on drying. So how could I not wish to continue enjoying this? You have taken years off me!

'But before we say another word, it is surely high time for a formal introduction.'

He put out a hand to Syd, and the younger man made to stand up.

'No, no, please stay put! You look so much more *au fait* down there than in these chintzy old chairs. And besides, I rather like having you seated at my feet. Not – it goes without saying – that this betokens any form of discipleship!'

Syd reached over and grasped his proffered hand.

'Morgan Forster,' said the seated man, doffing an imaginary cap as he met Syd's firm grip with gentle pressure of his own. 'What a cold hand you have! All the better for making pastry, I am given to understand. I am most glad to meet you, Mr – '

'Roger Barrett, sir.'

'Oh now, we must dispense with all these "sirs"! You shall call me Morgan.'

'Well – I will, then. Thank you.'

With their hands still locked, they appeared becalmed.

'Then you are no longer Syd?' Morgan asked.

Syd's gaze fell to the other man's arm, stretched across his own chest.

'Roger's my true name. It's what my family's always called me. Roger. Rodge.'

Morgan smiled and released his hand.

'You know,' he said, 'This is peculiar, but ever since that young fellow identified you as Syd, the name has seemed to me less and less – how shall I put it? – inapplicable to you. It is only a name. But – '

'No,' Syd interrupted, 'it's more than a name.'

He said this with conviction but gave no supporting detail, nor after a weighty pause did Morgan ask him to.

The author's eyes fell instead to the cigarette pack clutched in Syd's left fist. Then with all the firmness of a parent telling a child to eat up its greens he said to him: 'I strongly suggest you now smoke.'

Syd tapped the solitary cigarette half way out of the pack.

'Are you sure you don't want this?' he asked, holding it out.

Morgan gave a benevolent shake of the head, though not at once.

'We could – ' Syd continued. 'I mean, if you wanted to, we could share it?'

Morgan feigned a look of prim shock then decisively he patted the arm of his chair.

'Please do go ahead. Use my sherry glass down there for your ash. I am still, after my fashion, getting my breath back.'

Syd swivelled where he sat and reached behind himself to try to catch a light from the fire which now glowed amber through the vestiges of the collapsed logs of his chevron.

On succeeding, he swung back round and crossed his ankles where he sat.

He and Morgan were not quite sitting side by side – their feet were inches apart, their shoulders separated by a yard – but they gave an impression of being spectators, of looking on companionably in the expectation of some kind of floor show soon to be mounted in the room's far corner, between the piano and the desk by the window.

For several minutes neither man spoke, with Syd's smoke languidly swathing them. Then after a glance down to his right, Morgan said:

'You are looking across at my desk, where you may have seen I was sorting old photographs while also feeding honey to my moth?

'And if you are wondering if that wallah decked out in Indian garb is me – yes it is. In the early 1920s I worked for the Maharaja of Dewas as his private secretary. I look of course an absolute fright!'

Syd nodded. It was true that his gaze had been in the desk's direction, though he could just as easily have been trying to pick out through the murk the small painted budgerigar.

'Dassera!' Morgan then exclaimed, with such vim that the younger man gave a start.

When Syd frowned up, Morgan crossed his arms over his chest in a theatrical little shiver.

'At around this stage of the year, the opening of the cold weather season, there falls a Hindu festival. Dassera – or was it Dessera? A torchlit procession, all manner of other high jinks.

'In 1921 it fell to me to officiate as a kind of priest at the Dewas ceremonies. One was required to wave incense, sprinkle water and to dab with red powder anything that one liked.'

He paused to swallow a fond little smile.

'Under the direction of my clerk, I worshipped a pen, an inkpot and a wastepaper basket. As I remember it, a sacrament of coconut was offered. No words needed saying, and my Christian belief having by then long since disintegrated, I rather enjoyed myself.'

He paused. Clearly it was just a pause. Syd nodded, giving him the floor.

'As a grown man, I lacked the necessary sense of sin to follow Christ, d'you see? He seemed to me, besides, to lack a sense of humour, at least in so far as one could tell from the Bible.'

Syd continued to nod.

In other men of Morgan's age and uncertain health this could have been taken for wittering. Yet even as he made apparently idle chat he seemed also to be selecting each word as shrewdly as a seasoned shopper picking over all the apples in a tray before making his choice. And Syd, who had thawed considerably since Morgan's near-fall, may have reflected that it took a rare kind of genius even to witter with precision.

'One always hesitates to use one's own experience as evidence of anything,' Morgan went on, 'but much of what I found in the East helped me to complete my last novel, as mentioned earlier, which finally saw the light of day in 1924.'

'*A Passage to India*?' Syd tentatively asked rather than stated, and although they were no longer in each other's line of sight, Morgan nodded as if this were a given.

'I bring that up,' he went on, 'only to illustrate to you how long it can take for some work to achieve its finished form. That book was with me for some eleven years. Half your own lifetime!

'Not, I should hasten to say, that I worked at it continuously.'

The spry little laugh that followed really could have been a sneeze.

'It was as if something inside me was inciting me to dawdle and not to concentrate! Then there was the Great War, which of course slowed everyone down. But at so many points along the way I was convinced that it would never be written, and indeed, that no further novel at all ever would be written by me.

'And yet then there it was.'

Syd said nothing.

Little more than the filter of his cigarette remained. He turned the live end inward, as if he might be about to stigmatise his own palm, then he half swung away towards the hearth and tossed it into the fire.

'Within a couple of years of its publication,' Morgan continued, as if going off at a fresh tangent, 'I was able with the proceeds of its American sale to buy myself a little copse close to where I then lived.

'Nothing to rival the Hundred Acre Wood, you understand? Just the tiniest thing, but it did bring me acute joy. Oh, to hear the song made by the breeze through its leaves. The breath of life itself!'

He stopped short, head at a tilt, as if he still picked up faint strains.

'You cannot have spent long grappling with your new music,' Morgan reminded Syd. 'Is it not a little soon to be thinking in terms of the Cam?'

When Syd remained silent, Morgan said in a tone that implied this really had to be the last word on the subject:

'I do think we should leave all the drowning to poor Percy

Shelley. Just twenty-nine when we lost him. And what a loss! Quite, quite dreadful – '

Syd was looking up at him less guardedly than before. 'You did finally complete that novel,' he said. 'But didn't you say you haven't written another one since?'

Morgan clapped his hands together.

'Oh, how wonderful conversation is when the speaker means what he says and the listener attends!'

Syd smiled.

'So what's been happening since 1924?' he asked.

Morgan sat straighter in his seat, and made a pass at shooting his cuffs.

'We may conceivably come back to the subject of me,' he answered, 'should we need to. But at present it is your own enquiry we must address.

'I do not mean in regard to your painting. Rather your broader enquiry. One you have touched upon, while not yet perhaps framing it in so many words.'

Morgan smiled and raised a finger to show it had been his intention to sound gnomic, and Syd's struggle to understand was just as candid on his own face.

'You have not,' Morgan went on, 'asked for the first of my two reasons for soldiering on when life appeared to me unliveable, the beauty of nature having been the second.'

To invite an answer, Syd raised both eyebrows.

'It consisted of one word. "Selfish".'

Syd maintained his quizzical expression.

'We have referred already to the torments that the loss

of a child must bring to any parent. But I am thinking now not only of your mother, so near to us here at her home in Hills Road.

'Did you not bring up, a short while ago, a "girlfriend" – ?'

Syd opened his mouth as if to remonstrate, then immediately closed it and shook his head.

'You are no longer courting the girl?'

Morgan's eyes showed compassion.

'But I daresay there is someone else? The "gods" of your musical world must be spoiled for choice. The ardours of youth and what have you!'

Syd looked down and fed the empty cigarette pack around and around between the fingers of both hands, the picture of a man on the point of disclosure.

'I'm not – ' Syd began with a new half-smile.

'Well this may sound far-fetched, but I don't know if I've ever really chosen anyone. In that way. It seems – These things just usually seem to happen.

'Usually and often,' he said as an afterthought, still turning the pack but more slowly. 'Rather too often. For a time it became – disorderly.'

'But now?'

'I end up with girls who aren't right,' Syd continued as if this were an answer. 'Good girls. They couldn't be better – But never quite right. For me.

'I don't – I can't say I really know how to make a go of things. In order to make it last, that is. Not as Syd.

'And it's only really as Syd that I've been with girls.'

Setting down the pack upright on the floor in front of him, he ceased all movement with his hands.

'I've sometimes wondered,' he said, colour rising in his cheeks as he looked up and out into the room, 'whether it might have been better if I'd been a girl myself.'

'Better?'

He smiled and flexed his shoulders inside the tight red jacket through which the knuckles of his backbone showed whenever he hunched forward.

'Maybe I should have tried boys,' he said. 'Instead.'

Morgan stayed silent for a moment. Then he coughed as if to stifle inappropriate laughter.

'Are we alluding to the unspeakable vice of the Greeks?' he asked, the smile in his voice unsuppressed. 'The impulse that destroyed the City of the Plain? – '

Syd looked his way and they shared a stoical look of amusement.

'I don't know,' Syd admitted, returning his attention to the small empty pack.

'I possibly never will.'

Morgan allowed time for this new information to sink in – as new perhaps to the man who had just delivered it as to him who heard it. Then he cleared his throat.

'But I repeat my question: you have not, as yet, found for yourself "the" person?

'By that I mean a person whose pain would be as great as your mother's, were they to lose you now? "A mistress or a friend", as the poet has it, whom you have selected from the crowd, to travel "by the broad highway of the world"?'

'Which poet is that?' asked Syd.

'The fellow we lost so young to storms and bad seamanship in the Ligurian Sea: Shelley. And I should add that Shelley in his *Epipsychidion*, from which I have just quoted, is not recommending any kind of marriage. Oh, quite the opposite!'

A series of Morgan's short merry gasps caused Syd to look up at him.

'He refers with rather more approval to that crowd of "fair and wise" ones who make up a person's original circle – people who then as a rule must make way for "one chained friend, perhaps a jealous foe"!'

Syd smiled, his gaze falling to the gold ring on Morgan's finger as he rearranged his hands in his lap.

'*Epipsychidion* – ' he echoed appreciatively.

'A happy term, isn't it?' said Morgan. '"Concerning a little soul" might be its translation.

'But if you are presently still to settle upon "the" person, are there not others to whom you are close? A circle of the "fair and wise"?

'The people in your musical group, for instance? You said there was no war between you? You no longer perform with them, but you see them socially?'

Syd's face darkened. He put a hand to his neck chain. There was no need for him to make a verbal answer.

Morgan sniffed.

'Musical collaboration has its difficulties,' he said. 'I know as much from my own limited experience.'

With a glance across at the piano, Syd let go of his chain.

'What sort of collaboration was that?'

'Oh, nothing to change the course of musical history. I was invited to help with the libretto for an opera, that is all. Based upon Herman Melville's nautical story *Billy Budd*. There was a certain awkwardness while we worked together.'

'Really?' said Syd. 'Who wrote the score?'

'Oh!' Airily Morgan waved a hand. 'Ben Britten, as it happens. A dear friend. It was a rushed job for the Festival of Britain. They probably only came to me because no one else was available –

'But with you and your friends, there really was no big quarrel?'

Syd ran a hand through his hair.

'No quarrel I was aware of. I probably – Well, I think I just became less committed to the whole thing than the others. I'm – I'm not sure I always made it to our shows. It must have been very trying for them.

'And one of the old friends I'd known since school – He came in – I suppose you could say it was to deputise. There were four of us to start with, you see, then five.'

He bit on his lip.

'Then there were four again, whenever I was – indisposed.

'Until finally one time – I think it was this January, around my birthday – I was waiting for them to come and pick me up from my flat –

'I was quite prepared. I wasn't always, but I was that day. We were supposed to be driving down to play somewhere on the south coast, I believe. And – well, they just didn't come. To pick me up.'

After waiting for him to go on, Morgan's curiosity got the better of him.

'You didn't telephone them? Or try to travel to the engagement under your own steam?'

Syd splayed out both sets of fingers in front of him and grinned.

'I think I was beyond telephoning,' he said, not without

some sadness. 'Beyond steam.'

Then just as Morgan reached down to offer his shoulder a consolatory touch, Syd shifted slightly closer as if he were the older man's cat, or familiar.

'It's all right now,' Syd said, his voice finding a lower, audibly steadier register as Morgan took back his arm after the briefest of contact.

'I'm all right. About that. We'd run our course. I mean, it had been three years. There was nothing more there –

'I think they'll probably just forget all about me.'

Morgan caught his breath. 'I very much doubt that.'

'But I am all right.'

'We shan't have another Shelley on our hands?' asked Morgan. 'At least not for the time being? I accept that it really is too much to expect a man to change his life's direction in the course of one late afternoon.'

Syd leaned his shoulder against the chair leg, pressing the flat of his left hand against the floorboards close to Morgan's right, brogue-shod foot.

A moment or two later, as if nothing could have been more natural, he lifted the hand, closed it lightly over the older man's shoe and left it there.

'Perhaps it's you,' Syd Barrett respectfully suggested, 'who should now stop talking about death – '

Morgan chortled.

'Ah, but death can be turned to such good use, can it not? Creatively?'

His own voice had dropped into a deeper, more mellow reach of its range, and Syd tilted his head, considering what this question might mean.

The new resonance in Morgan's voice might have allowed him to quote in illustration one of his own *bons mots*: "Death destroys a man, but the idea of death saves him".

Instead with characteristic modesty he said:

'This is something we might now usefully go on to discuss – '

'Would you perhaps care to listen to some music while we talk?' asked Morgan. 'There is a gramophone over there. Though my discs do not stray very far from Beethoven, I am afraid.'

Syd's hold on Morgan's foot grew marginally tighter.

'No, I – No, the peace in here is very pleasing.'

'Provided our man upstairs keeps his radio down!'

Syd relaxed his grip then slid his hand away but its edge stayed in touch with Morgan's thick mud-speckled sole.

He positioned his chin on his own raised left knee, some pale skin of which was showing through a threadbare patch in his jeans.

There was no denying the room's quietness, charged though it was with many echoes of what they both had so freely said already.

There seemed now to be more space inside it too, as if the pair of them were looking out across a vast expanse of shore left uncovered by a retreating tide – an old man sunk deep in his deckchair with his still-growing grandson, perhaps, tucked in by his side.

*

'I was arrested,' Morgan recommenced, 'by something you said earlier.

'It was about, for want of a better term, your "lost inspiration". You said rather nicely that first there was nothing, then something, then nothing again.

'Immediately that struck a chord in my mind but I could not quite think why. Now I have it. It is Bede and his sparrow, d'you see?

'Somewhere in his *Ecclesiastical History of the English People*, Bede writes of a conversation between a Saxon king and his councillors. They are debating whether or not to adopt Christianity, as they are being advised to by some tiresome missionary.

'This would have been almost a millennium and a half ago. And one of the king's men compares the current, pagan perception of human life to a sparrow's flight through a warm and well-lit feasting hall in winter.

'In through one door the sparrow flies then out through the other, almost comet-like – or at least in the way comets were regarded during the pre-scientific era. That is all we know of her: this brief period of her passage, while to either side, all is darkness and unknowing. Where she came from, where she is going – no one can possibly say.'

'It is a similar mystery,' Syd agreed.

'The parallels are imperfect,' said Morgan, 'and had I been one of the councillors I should have suggested that the king pack off that Christian missionary with a flea in his ear – but the apparent arbitrariness in Bede's imagery is what speaks to me now.

'The sparrow may fly through the hall at any point in one's creative life. There is no telling how much darkness may precede it, nor how much may follow, nor how often the bucket may come up empty.'

'But you do see it as darkness?' Syd asked. 'The times when one isn't creating?'

'This is what I wish to come to,' Morgan replied.

'No, I don't believe that I do. I really am not at all convinced that this is the case.'

Morgan stretched out a leg in the direction of the book which still lay on the floor ahead of them.

'Take Grahame here, for instance. The fate of his son of course cast intolerable shadows over the latter part of his life. But in purely literary terms it was not all darkness, either before or after he produced that single work for which he is most revered.

'And he produced it relatively early in his life too. Others may well have badgered him to write more in the same vein, or even just more at all. The author himself knew where he stood. You know his stout answer when he was challenged to be more prolific?'

Syd shook his head.

'"I am a spring, not a pump"!'

Morgan's shoulders heaved though he made no sound as he laughed.

'A A Milne, whose fame affected his own son Christopher Robin terribly negatively, and who also of course adapted Grahame's work for the stage, showed similar reluctance to add to his *Pooh* canon. He grew most annoyed by the clamour that he should do so, claiming he wished to escape from children's books altogether, his complaint being that England expects the writer, like the cobbler, to stick to his last!

'Although possibly a better example of youthful achievement followed by more than half a lifetime of non-production is that of our splendid Rimbaud, who came and went as a poet before the age of twenty-one!

'One's *floruit* need not be long. That is the text for this miniature sermon of mine. And there is good life to be lived on either side.'

'*Floruit*?' repeated Syd.

'A Latin tag denoting a peak period of activity. That of an artist or movement. It simply means "he flourished".

'One's own *floruit* is, in retrospect, extremely short. My first novel, or rather novelette, was published in 1905. And then as I keep telling you, after the *Passage* it was all up. Less than twenty fertile years, leaving almost seven of my decades unaccounted for, at least in terms of fiction. And even within those twenty were some fourteen fallow years!'

'And did you always intend to write?' asked Syd for a second time. 'I mean, you must have been in your twenties when your novelette – '

'Twenty-six. A quite extraordinarily unworldly twenty-six to boot. My word – a primrose indeed not yet picked!'

'But did you – ? Was it – Was writing what you always thought you were – well – for?'

*

Morgan puffed out his cheeks and with a good-hearted little groan he retracted the foot pointing towards *The Wind in the Willows*.

'It is all so very long ago. But there did not seem to be much else. My tripos result here was undistinguished, so academia did not beckon. And as an only child I had my mother to look out for. I had no large ambitions in any direction, I believe. But I had become friendly with my classics tutor – a squat man with a dreary voice called Wedd, who at one time kept this very room as part of his set.'

Morgan smiled to himself.

'Nathaniel Wedd had a particularly foul mouth. He would spit when he saw the procession into Chapel!

'And one day he casually mentioned to me that he really saw no reason why I shouldn't write. I suppose I must have taken his suggestion on board, since there were always going to be readers with an appetite for stories about the love of men for women, and vice-versa –

'But the reasons why we favour one course of action over another are seldom simple. There are many ways of being alive, many doors near to one which someone else's touch may open.'

Chewing on his lower lip, the younger man gave a nod but he seemed distracted.

'I'm just trying to work it out – ' Syd said.

'You told me that you'd had – didn't you say? – a crisis when you were about my age.

'So was it about what you should do with your life at that point? How you might best express who you were? – '

Still smiling at his recollections of Wedd, Morgan carefully weighed the question.

'I would say no to the first part of your question,' he finally decided, 'but yes to the second. It had, however, little to do with the subject of creativity. Therefore I see no cause for this to detain us here – '

Catching a sharp new strangled quality in his voice, Syd looked up.

Morgan did not meet his eye. He couldn't. His own eyes had become brimful of tears.

'No, of course,' said Syd.

'Of course – '

While Morgan again made use of his handkerchief, Syd unfurled himself, stretching his arms above his head and pushing himself on to his feet.

He glanced back at the fire, as if to check that it didn't require more building up. Then in open admiration he looked around the room, at its manifold elements all in their rightful place, a lifetime's jigsaw now complete.

To stretch his legs he stepped forward, over Kenneth Grahame's book with its still-unconsulted seventh chapter, the chapter in which the animal comrades Rat and Mole finally locate the Otter's wayward son, safe and well, after tracking to its source the most miraculous music either of them has ever heard.

Syd crossed to the desk in that part of the room on which both men had been training their eyes.

He took another cursory look at the portrait of the doe-eyed Morgan in his Indian outfit, turban and all, back in the Roaring Twenties. But this time he made no secret of his interest in the little green budgerigar.

Morgan laughed affectionately.

'It is one of a pair,' he said. 'Gifts from India. Although I believe the budgerigar is native to Australia. A place in which

I have never set foot, and probably now never shall.

'You may handle it if you wish – '

With some ceremony Syd did so, picking it up with his right hand and setting it down square on the flattened palm of his left. Then he breathed the word 'budgerigar', drawing it out as earlier he had said *Epipsychidion*, a man for whom language still held a child's wonder.

'Such a long word for so tiny a creature,' Morgan agreed with a tired and slightly vague smile.

'And I understand that the nomadic birds of their species who live in the wild are considerably smaller than those bred in captivity. Not that they need to be any larger. They have made a pretty good fist of surviving for five million years!'

Syd raised the stridently painted bird just above his eye level and ducked his unkempt head to look at its breast from below.

'It's – It really is very good,' he said, replacing it exactly where he had found it on the desk, like a chalice upon an altar.

He looked back with uncertainty at the very old and frail author whose eyes he had so recently caused to fill with tears.

'I do think I'm overtaxing you, though – ' he said.

Morgan waved away all such concerns.

'Overtaxing is another interesting word,' he said, pointing a finger as if at its vanishing echo.

'One seldom finds oneself undertaxed. Just as a person nowadays is much more likely to be described as underprivileged. Naturally I do not refer to the likes of ourselves in this respect.'

He shot a tart look at Syd, who shifted from foot to foot beside the desk.

'I myself – and from what I gather, you too – have been landed with more privilege than one truly knows what to do with. Thanks to a family legacy I have been "comfortably off" ever since I went about in little girl's clothing. Not that we are to be blamed for our good fortune. It enables us, as subversives, to open the establishment's gates from within!

'But this idea of being "underprivileged" intrigues me. Lacking in such advantages as can accrue only to the few!

'No, my boy, I am far from overtaxed. Your visit invigorates me! And for that I thank the man at the BBC.'

Syd nodded.

'He did say you were open to visitors – '

'"Open to visitors"! One is not a public convenience!

'But this man – he was employed by the Corporation? I have put in a certain amount of time there myself over the years. I may know him?'

Syd wrinkled his nose.

'No, I don't believe – No, he didn't have a position there. He was just visiting. He ran into me as I was coming out –

'I think he was in the music field too. Some sort of an impresario.

'I only saw him that one time.'

He paused then, abruptly, as if making a mental note to verify this later, and he went on as if faintly puzzled.

'A big man, he was. Not really a city type – ' He put up a hand and gave his chin a cursory stroke. 'Little beard.'

Morgan assimilated all this with the flicker of a smile.

'No matter,' he replied. 'But yes, yes – my door is generally not closed. This college is already something of a thoroughfare, but if someone makes a point of seeking me out, I try to be available. They come from all over, you know?'

'But at least,' he said after a pause, 'tucked away up here I am not, as it were, on public view. Unlike certain other, more august writers – '

He narrowed his eyes as if assessing whether or not to be indiscreet, the smile from before lingering at the corners of his mouth.

'While writing the *Passage* I paid several visits to old Thomas Hardy and his wife, down on the outskirts of Dorchester. They kept a very grand home but charabancs would whizz past outside and the conductor would cry out to his passengers, "'Ome of Thomas 'Ardy, Novelist"!'

Both men laughed.

'The Hardys found it a trial,' Morgan said, trying not to splutter.

'Like his work, Hardy's company yielded few opportunities for laughter. He once gave me a guided tour of the graves of all their cats. A very great number of graves, overgrown with ivy, the cats' names inscribed on headstones. Apparently there had been more cats still, whose bodies had not been recovered.

'And here is the nub: most of them seemed to have been run over by trains – '

He checked himself, losing his battle not to seem frolicsome in the face of tragedy.

'So I asked Hardy if a railway line ran nearby, and he said to me, "Not at all near, not at all near – I don't know how it is"!

'Oh, oh, one really shouldn't – '

He gave two of his tiny sneezes, and again dabbed at his eyes with the handkerchief, while Syd at the desk-side stood lit up by gentle laughter too.

'Oh dear me, I have talked again of death,' cried Morgan as he straightened himself out. 'In spite of your reprimand.

'You do, if I may say so, have the most devastating smile.

'Is that why you unleash it so infrequently?'

He flicked a wrist toward the desk against which Syd now leaned his hip.

'Please do pull out that chair. Make yourself as comfortable as you can. And oh, your hand does look depleted without something to smoke. I only wish I kept some cigarettes here to offer you.

'Sit, please sit, and let us return to the subject of your work – '

As Syd drew out from beneath the desk its intricately carved chair, which may well have been a Chippendale with a newly upholstered seat, his gaze took in for a moment the roll-up in the mantelpiece niche.

He turned the chair to face Morgan across the rug and perched himself.

'My work – ?' he asked with a sigh.

'Your work, yes. Your music, in the first instance.'

Morgan had begun to play with his hands, pulling with some fretfulness at the tip of one finger after another as if he were plucking off invisible washing-up gloves.

Although still expressive, his fingers seemed stiff, resistant. His piano-playing days now had to be behind him, this man who had let it be known that upon learning of the outbreak of war in 1939 at the age of sixty he had for a short while wept alone, then set himself the task of working sequentially through Beethoven's sonatas.

'For a person still as young as yourself,' Morgan proposed, 'progress is to be measured not in years but months. At this particular time you may lack the sense of a solid mass ahead, but it is surely too soon to step down from your place in the pantheon of musical gods?

'In addition, it would seem to be the ancillary aspects of the music world that exasperate you. The work as commodity. Whereas for you – as for me – it is rather the amateur spirit which appeals.

'Let us then think more about creative endeavour itself. Have you ruled out collaboration of any kind? That is, after all, what you are used to, with your group.

'Your man Lennon, for instance, whom you hold in such high regard – would you be able to pool your talents with his?'

For two heartbeats Syd looked as if he had been punched on the side of the head. He smiled.

'No, that's – No, I understand he's just found someone else to collaborate with. She's an artist, actually. An interesting one.'

'Very well. Then you say you are aiming to find a setting for some verses of Joyce. This sounds promising. What else do you have on the stocks?'

Syd crossed his ankles under the chair.

'I – Well, what I've mainly been doing in the studio is jamming. Improvising. To see what might emerge.'

'Yes?'

'But I've also been – I might also try to set to music some lyrics I wrote a little while back. An Edward Lear kind of a poem.

'No, an attempt at a pastiche of Belloc really – '

Morgan cupped his ear. 'I beg your pardon?'

'Hilaire Belloc?'

'Ah! You enjoy a little humorous English wordplay?'

'I do – though you'd hardly think it, would you, listening to me today?'

Morgan gave an away-with-you flip of his eighty-nine-year-old hand.

'You have the Comic Muse hard by your shoulder,' he assured Syd. Then cryptically he murmured, 'I saw him,' before going on:

'Belloc of course, could not have been more different from Grahame, in the sense that no one was able to stop that man writing. When asked why he was so prolific, do you know what he said?'

Syd didn't.

'"Because my children are howling for pearls and caviar"!'

Morgan gasped with glee. 'At least you and I are not under

pressure from that quarter. Or I assume that you are not?'

After the briefest of pauses Syd shook his head.

'A piece of whimsy, is it,' Morgan resumed, 'your pastiche?'

'Just a sort of squib really. It's – Well actually it's about a scare-mongering elephant. He gets eaten by a tiger, on whose account he'd previously put the entire jungle on red alert.'

Syd fingered his neck chain in deep unease.

'It's not exactly going to be Beethoven,' he added. 'Or Britten.'

'This accompanying music shall be psychedelic?'

'Oh no, I don't really – No, I think that's passed over now. That kind of – that school of music. I'd personally prefer to keep things simpler.'

In silence Morgan brought his palms together.

'I am trying to recall for you what Hemingway says. Is it that "the world breaks everyone and afterward many are strong in the broken places"?

'This may apply as you go on.

'I am also reminded of something I spotted not long ago while leafing through my own commonplace book. In 1932, at the age of fifty-three, I noted that during the previous two years I had been happy. I had not been expecting to be happy, but I was. It is possible, d'you see, for happiness to come in one's natural growth?

'I wanted, at that time, to remind others that their turns too can come. I do not have many messages to give, but this seemed to me to be one well worth passing on. And I am not sure that I did it then, but I am telling you now.'

He exhaled as if relieved of a burden.

'The world can offer great chances of beauty and adventure. As you put it yourself: one never knows what might emerge.'

Syd shifted from side to side, placing his hands palm down beneath his thighs.

'But what if nothing does?' he asked.

'Now this too is a fascinating question,' Morgan replied.

'I know it has been said of me that my reputation rises with every novel I haven't written. And an early "retirement" in any artistic field does relieve the artist of the need to negotiate mediocrity! – '

'But in comparison with you,' Syd argued, 'what I've produced so far is dreadfully thin – '

Morgan raised a finger.

'You may say that, but do those who now hail your divinity say the same? More pertinently, will those who are not yet born say it?'

Syd had to smile at the idea that any future generation would take more than a passing interest in mid-1960s pop.

'I am not saying this will surely happen,' Morgan told him. 'But at the turn of this century, little did I expect my own thin offerings to endure. We throw forth our work to the world, and there it must have its own life: the genie in the open air.

'The novel of mine I am most glad to have written, for instance, turns out to be my least popular! You may not even have heard of it – *The Longest Journey*, its title lifted from Shelley's *Epipsychidion*, just as *A Passage to India* comes from Whitman.'

He jerked his thumb again at the Picasso reproduction.

'But as he reminds us, "Art is theft"!

'We can only guess what may happen during the rest of this century, and on into the next. But let me make this suggestion – and such are the musings of idle old men shut away in their ivory towers: I have sometimes wondered whether it suits one's devotees that one has ceased to produce!'

He returned Syd's sceptical smile with a more sprightly one of his own.

'Our legends become lacquered in interesting ways,' he explained. 'You mentioned when speaking of musical messiahs that your public seems all too interested in what you and your fellow performers "stand for". This may not be restricted to music.

'For many, I myself have seemed for some while to stand for Edwardian England – an era with which, incidentally, as a younger man I felt entirely out of joint!

'But the England of King Edward VII is where much of my fiction is set, so that is what I and my novels have come to denote to people. For them, I embody an Age – and who knows, there may be something in that?

'But, do you see? What I represent matters more to them than what I am, and this gives me a form of tenure. To that extent, had I written more novels in the Thirties, Forties and Fifties – regardless of their quality, and quality is dashed difficult to maintain, by the by – then some of my *cachet*, for what that is worth, may have been lost.'

He reached up and gave a tug to his walrus moustache.

'And you may call what I am about to say even more misguided,' he continued, although in truth Syd was staring across at him now with neither smile nor frown, 'but in the event that nothing more should emerge after you have sent down your bucket a few more times, it is not impossible that whether you wish to leave a mark or not, your own legacy may already be assured.'

With that, Syd did grin, not in the devastating way Morgan had remarked on earlier, rather a rictus of plain disbelief.

'In the minds of those who lionise you, henceforth you and your music may long be associated with our current era in the onward march of England's story. And people do have long memories. When Clement Attlee was Prime Minister after the second war I was offered a knighthood for work I had largely completed before the first!'

Syd nodded. 'Did you accept it?'

'No, no, no. What would I have been wanting with such a trinket? And besides, being a "Sir" would have put up my bills!

'No, no. If they are still handing out honours so arbitrarily in fifty years time, and one can hardly imagine they will, then you too may be given a gong! All they mean is that one was once in the public eye and is not yet dead.'

'My point is that you may not be required to produce further work, at least not for them. Which would leave you free to express your creativity perhaps in other areas.'

'Free, as long as I live at home with my mother?'

'Would she not be delighted to have you back?'

'Well – probably.

'Well yes, I'm sure she would – But – '

Morgan leaned forward with a shake of the head to silence him, the bit now firmly between his teeth.

'You do,' he said, 'grasp my less flippant argument?

'At the risk of bringing up death yet again, you suggested that your followers wanted you to die for them but without dying. That may in fact not only be possible, it may provide the best solution for all concerned.

'When the time comes, you could go into a form of internal exile, and conduct your business in virtually total privacy, once again as Roger, while for your *aficionados* you will still be Syd. Just as I for so long have conducted my business as Morgan rather than "E M Forster", leading the life I choose, with no one outside my immediate circle any the wiser.'

Syd gave a wry smile.

'You make this other life of yours sound mysterious,' he said. 'As if you're keeping something hidden – '

Morgan disregarded that.

'To these followers,' he persisted, 'what one was, I have found, is much more important than what one is. Their perception will always be of you as you were, during the period of your *floruit*. It is a notion for which logic offers little support, but for them, you may never grow any older.

'And is not immortality, after all, the very least that a god might expect!'

Syd uncrossed his ankles and swung his legs beneath the seat, perhaps delaying his response until he'd gauged quite how seriously Morgan intended him to take this.

'And here is the rub,' said Morgan. 'These admirers of ours have no option but to grow older themselves. Yet through their endorsement they give us the chance, if we so wish it, to stay young!

'I do not of course mean in the physical sense. My own sorry decrepitude is proof of that. More in the manner of not having to put away childish things, keeping our younger selves intact, for better or for worse. Absolving us from at least some of the more irksome responsibilities of adulthood – again, if we so wish.

'For while others go about their daily lives in such professions as your ancillary aspects of the music world – professions which I am sure must bring their own rewards – we, like the gilded children we are, are permitted to go on dreaming.

'No, it may be even more than this! Is it possible that they need us to continue to dream on their behalf? Is this the tacit transaction?'

Syd shook his head, in perplexity rather than denial.

'But – ' he remonstrated. 'But you didn't. Yourself.'

Morgan's smile became quizzical. He tilted his head to hear more.

'I mean,' said Syd, 'if that is the transaction, then in your case, you didn't – I mean, you haven't – You haven't actually gone on dreaming.'

He smiled at the older man, as devastatingly as he was able.
'Have you?'

Morgan closed his eyes.

His eyes stayed closed.

He was either about to suffer another of his turns, or else he was gathering himself to say something which required even longer prior deliberation than usual.

'Before I ever started *Passage*, but once I had completed *Howards End*,' he then said, sooner than Syd might have anticipated, his eyes more firmly shut, 'I made a start on something new. It was a novel. You know, the usual form – the love of men for women and vice-versa?'

Slowly his eyes opened, but they remained hooded and there was little, if any, liveliness in them.

Syd nodded at him to go on. Clearly the older man had made a decision to cease hedging in certain areas and speak out.

'But my heart – ' Morgan said. 'My heart was not really in it. So I abandoned it, and in time the idea for the *Passage* came to me – I have described how tortuous a process writing that book became.

'But after it was finished, there was another development.

'I considered embarking on further fiction. Of course I did. This was my *metier*. I wished to write a story which addressed the only serious theme worth treating, that of two people pulling each other into salvation, since I happen to believe that it takes two to make a Hero – '

He looked more searchingly at Syd, across the small green book that lay between them on the floor.

'And you may be assured that plenty of others gave me every encouragement to put pen to paper once more. No one was holding a gun to my head. Nothing like that. But even the back covers of my earlier Penguin editions used to describe me as "all too reticent" as a novelist – '

His voice dropped. Again, tantalisingly, he seemed to be on the point of disengagement.

'Was it – ?' Syd hazarded. 'Did it seem too much like "obligatory creation"?'

Morgan gave a tiny shiver, as if the very phrase still haunted him.

'The act of creation itself presented no problem. My reluctance concerned what I was writing about.

'For what did I know – truly know – about my subject? I who had never found myself in such a position, never married – '

His voice threatened to break and he came up so short that Syd, still sitting on the backs of his pastry-friendly hands like a primary school pupil at morning assembly, was driven to fill the silence.

'You never married?'

Morgan's eyes remembered then how to dance.

'Oh,' he said, 'I think anyone married to me would have found themselves straining against the bonds of matrimony within hours!'

He peered at the shoe over which Syd had so unaffectedly closed his hand.

'I never married, no,' he said as if in wonder.

'And I had known that I never should marry – ever since

that time to which I have already referred, when I was much the same age as you are now. It was in 1902, and I received a revelation about myself.'

He folded his hands in his lap.

'One which caused me, at first, to question my commitment to life. One which made me think that I too was hearing the call of the Cam.'

Footsteps could be heard on the staircase outside, somebody's light skip gathering volume down to the level of Morgan's landing, the sound then dissolving into the darkness below.

Morgan girded himself to say what he had to.

'The important thing, Roger, is to swim with the tide of one's own being.'

He took a ragged breath and began to shake his head.

'The love of men for women, you see – '

Before he could go on, Syd pushed himself up on to his feet.

In the colder shadows he suddenly looked extremely tall, and not a little foreboding, perhaps even closer now in appearance to the avenging angel Morgan may first have imagined he had woken up to find. For a moment the air seemed visibly to brim, lap and course around his elemental figure.

'We are alluding to the unspeakable vice of the Greeks?' Syd asked.

Morgan lowered his gaze.

'I very much fear that we are.'

'Oh, Morgan – ' Syd breathed.

His expression softened and he came to where the old gentleman sat.

Kneeling beside him, he placed both his hands upon Morgan's to make him raise his head. Those aged eyes – the crow's feet at their corners tightening – were filled with uncried tears.

It was Morgan who then broke contact, withdrawing one hand to reach up and take off his glasses, the other to ferret in his pocket for his handkerchief.

'Sit by me where you were before,' he said brusquely, and Syd complied, again resting his half-closed left fist on the toe of Morgan's right brogue.

'I would rather you were not now in a position to look at me,' Morgan told him after blowing his nose with gusto. 'Lord, what fools we mortals be!'

'You're certainly no fool,' Syd said into the room's wide open spaces.

'Oh, I know what I am – what kind of primrose was waiting to be picked.

'And picked I finally was. Well and truly. In subsequent years I more than made up for lost time. Although, needless to say, my days of "feasting with panthers" are now some distance behind me.'

Syd smiled up, as Morgan had wanted him to.

'But has it been – ?' he asked. 'I mean, were you able to find love?'

Dampening his lips with his tongue Morgan turned his hands this way and that as if encouraging the fire to strike a glint of light from his simple golden signet ring.

'I have found people,' he said, clearly moved to have been asked.

'I have found people whom I have had the good luck to love, and the even better luck to be loved by in return.'

He closed his eyes.

'My greatest and most enduring love, a man thirty years my junior, lives at present in Coventry. We are, in our own fashion, still together.'

His eyelids fluttered open.

'He is married with a family – and they are all good people.

'When I spoke before of the loss of a son, it was to this family that I referred. In the year of your father's death, their son – my godchild – fell ill with Hodgkin's disease. Within a year he died. Nothing, for any of us, has since been quite the same.'

Morgan looked down and plucked compulsively at the trouser crease on his right leg. He took a long breath.

'The man lunching with me at the pub out Milton way was not, as you will now appreciate, my son.

'I imagine the person at the BBC who told you otherwise knew that too.'

He smiled, oddly.

'One almost might say, about this person at the BBC, that he was being a little devilish – '

For several minutes all was silent. But it was a silence of expectancy.

Both men sat with straighter backs than they had before, the way the more conventional men of King's would recently have been sitting in the Chapel across the front court, but with their own eyes trained on Picasso's horse and boy instead of an altar and an east window.

They sat as if needing to stay alert – not in case they should miss some spectacle spawning up out of all the literature and artistry before them, but rather their ears were cocked as if for a sound that might burst forth. And beyond the room, the River Cam ran shallow in comparison to what they listened for: those deeper waters which are likened in the *Book of Proverbs* to the words from men's mouths, the wellspring of wisdom described there as a flowing brook.

Morgan made a small dry sound at the back of his throat, suggesting he might be ready to speak further.

Keeping his eyes forward, Syd tilted his head to listen.

'You said,' Morgan began, 'when speaking about the tedious requirements made of you as a professional musician, that this was taking you into a different sort of conversation from the one you had imagined. I think I see what you mean.

'You had hoped to be heard in the great debate to which all creative artists contribute, the pooling of all the cases ever made through the ages? That conversation? The whole kit and caboodle!'

Syd said nothing for a moment.

'The world may seem to be in irreversible decline,' Morgan continued to rhapsodise, 'and our artists' contributions are indeed the fragments we shore against our ruin. True, all true.

'But oh, Roger, what speech or song they make in concert! It is the way in which we as a race have always made the best of one another!'

Deep in thought, Syd inclined his head a little more.

'In concert – yes perhaps,' he replied, moving his head from side to side as if to pick out in the room's turbid depths the shapes of the players of countless complementary instruments.

Self-consciously he smiled.

'I may – You know, I think I may once have heard something like that.'

His voice seemed to drop an octave.

'My sister says – I don't now remember this myself, but my sister tells me that when I was young I used to sit up in bed in the mornings and conduct imaginary orchestras. Just –

'Well, it was just out of the joy of being alive, I suppose.'

'Yes,' said Morgan Forster. 'Yes – '

Gently Morgan re-directed their own conversation:

'After producing five novels and a number of shorter stories about the love of men for women and vice-versa, there seemed little more that I myself could usefully contribute to such a debate.

'I had been making a case, it is true, but it was not my own case. And of course, in the world of that time – or should I say, the England? – the case I may have wished to make would not have been permitted.'

'Oh Morgan – ' Syd murmured a second time. 'So you stopped? Writing fiction?'

Morgan did not reply at once.

'I did not so much stop writing fiction. Not initially. Rather I stopped allowing what I wrote to be read. At least beyond a certain *coterie*.

'There is a novel put away in a safe place. A few further stories.'

He chuckled.

'When I am gone, there is a chance these may be allowed to see the light of night!

'But not before. Never before.'

He tapped his chest.

'I need to be disposed of first.'

'You said England wouldn't have let you make your case,' Syd put back to Morgan after another, shorter pause.

'Did you consider living somewhere else? Somewhere that might have been – freer?'

'Permanently?' asked Morgan with a little wistfulness. 'Oh, doubtless I could have found somewhere more congenial. I became aware of such places on my travels. But England, our England, for all its imperfections, prepared a niche for me and I have been reluctant to leave.

'It was upon these shores, after all, that I was granted my

little sip of pure creation, which in turn helped to re-create me, for the art cannot help but in some way change the artist!'

'A niche,' Syd echoed softly, sounding a little wistful himself.

Morgan sat up, as close to attention as he was able, then he smiled and raised both palms at the fathomless mystery.

'What possesses me to vouchsafe all this to you, a perfect stranger, I cannot be sure! It has not happened before. Yet for my own reasons I am glad it has happened. Very glad, and very grateful.'

Without dropping his hands, he tilted back his head as if to see clean through the ceiling and far into the star-encrusted infinities beyond.

'The reason I say grateful,' he told Syd, 'is that in your company not only has my tongue been loosened, but I have also found myself getting nearer in what I say – nearer than for a very long time – to what is in my mind. Or rather toward that junction of mind with heart, which is where the creative impulse sparks.

'I have felt today with you, often, that my speech is being prompted from without, but by one who knows what I need to say. It has made me feel both out of character and yet wholly myself.'

Syd tipped back his head, eyes closed, his hand attracted again to his neck chain.

'I've felt that too,' he said. 'Words put in my mouth, but the thoughts were all my own. It's almost at times been like – '

'Like what?'

Syd looked sheepish. 'As if I'm being played. You know, musically? As if, well, as if this whole thing has been – scored.'

Morgan smiled. 'So much in one's life does not bow to the known rules of nature,' he said. 'Our bodies may be England's, yet we are all but pulses in the eternal mind!

'And what is passing now through your own mind?'

'Right now?' asked Syd. 'Oh, I was just – I was still thinking about my old bedroom. The one where I would conduct the orchestras?'

'Go on.'

'There were three tetrahedrons there that I made from balsa wood, hanging by threads from the ceiling.

'I can – Still I can see them twisting. In the breeze. I loved to see them twist – '

Morgan nodded as if he too felt that breeze, a privately generated ripple of cleansing air that had coursed all the way across town from Hills Road to King's.

'Home thoughts are all to the good,' Morgan said, 'with your mother there to welcome you.'

'When you depart from here,' Morgan followed up after a short hiatus during which Syd opened his eyes, 'you will be going to see your mother?'

It sounded less of a question than a statement of fact.

'You know,' Syd replied, 'I was actually planning to visit her today anyway.

'I mean, I didn't set out to come here. I'd forgotten all about the guy at the BBC, and what he'd said, until – '

'Yes?'

'Well – '

He frowned, spooling back to the moment.

'I think it was when someone nearly ran me over in Silver Street. On a bike. Someone who must have reminded me of that BBC man – '

'An impresario, you called him?' said Morgan, nodding as if in corroboration.

Syd didn't give an answer. Nor did Morgan press for one. Instead in a slower, dreamier voice Syd reverted to his original point.

'I was on my way to see my mother,' he said, his features taking on a new melancholic set. 'Though I'm really not at all sure what I intended to do once I got there. Really not at all – '

'Ah, your mother!' said Morgan as if to jolly him along. 'She will greet you with the shout of the morning star!

'A woman's greeting is not to be under-estimated,' he quickly went on when Syd stayed silent. 'There is a very fine person here at King's – a Mrs Richardson, my bedmaker – whose spontaneous cry of delight whenever she sees me I regard as a precious gift. One that I would now set alongside any success I may have had in literature.'

He eyed Syd with mock severity.

'Your mother will also very likely set about feeding you up. You look to me as thin as one of your gramophone records.'

Syd's smile in reply was equivocal.

'And I am by no means trying to send you on your way at once,' Morgan concluded, 'but there is a dinner here in college tonight which I am obliged in due course to attend.'

As if roused by the prospect, a loud gurgling came from his stomach, which Morgan fondly patted like a waking pet.

'But when you do go, you should remember to take with you the items that spilled from your pockets out on the landing and were handed in by the servant.

'I placed them over there on the mantelpiece.

'Why don't you fetch them now, lest later you forget?'

Syd took longer to get to his feet than Morgan had before his near-fall.

He delayed even longer by going up onto his toes to stretch his calves. Morgan still looked out into the room – not to his side, where Syd now stood – and he seemed affably determined to go on doing so.

Syd turned away.

The fire had burned low but he declined to re-stock it. Briefly he may have entertained the idea of snatching up the joint along with the balled banknote, then surreptitiously palming the former into the foamy ash and glowing coals.

In the event, after a glance back at his benevolent host's profile, he retrieved and retained both.

'Come back now,' Morgan said, patting his own chair arm. 'There is still a little time before I must go to eat my beautiful soup!'

Syd took a step back towards him. Morgan turned his way and spoke again, a gleam in his eye.

'Smoke your cigarette, why don't you?' he said.

'You do not need to use the fire to light it. You will have

noticed a box of matches back there in the same niche – '

*

For Syd, there seemed no escape, no way to decline. His attempt at a smile faltered. This appeared to be a matter of principle to Morgan. He pointed a finger to reaffirm where Syd might find the matches.

Stuffing the banknote into his jacket pocket, Syd returned to the mantelpiece, his every move followed by Morgan.

'Sir, I think I should say,' Syd steeled himself to admit, 'this cigarette isn't – '

Morgan flapped a hand to silence him.

'Oh, sir, sir! I thought we had dispensed with your niceties!

'And I am perfectly aware of the properties of your cigarette! You must remember I have spent a good deal of my time in both the Far and Middle East, with their hashish dives, their opium dens!

'Please stop looking so bilious, and come back to your berth beside me. I am happy for you to take your ease. After such an extended reprieve from my normal condition, it will be a most appropriate celebration, since I gather that the substance of your cigarette is of medicinal value even to those who simply sit by while another smokes!'

Instead of sitting on the hard floor any longer, Syd drew from near the three-seater sofa a football-sized *pouffe* covered in a dark flowery fabric.

He perched himself upon it and took a mordant look at

the partly smoked joint.

With a final glance at Morgan, whose face was now almost on a level with his own and who gave him a firm nod of abetment, he lit up with little fuss. In fact he couldn't afford to draw a blank with the match since there were no others.

Syd left the matchbox open and balanced it on his left knee, the one nearer to Morgan, as an *ad hoc* ashtray.

Then a change began slowly to declare itself.

In the moments after Syd exhaled for the first time, the alteration in the room's atmosphere could not have gone unnoticed by either man.

As the gauzy, pale smoke wafted around them like pungent incense, a sense of some imminent sacrament gathered. And if their heads had been cocked in anticipation before, now an outside observer might have guessed from their expressions that a sound had indeed begun to swell up out of all those books, pictures and artefacts which stood as but a fragment of the world's wealth of art and learning, of insight and experience, of the lore of the ages that was freely available to anyone, like the two of them, with the passionate intentness to tune into it.

And the point of entry for them both lay in the thin, clear happy call of distant piping – if not the breath of life itself then nonetheless a crucial breath, a sound to be heard only with the heart, and so deeply that for as long as it lasted, the two of them were indeed this music.

At a certain point, as Syd eased some ash into the matchbox, he noticed that Morgan's right elbow had slid a short way off its arm rest.

But his forearm had not obeyed gravity by continuing to drop until his fingertips touched the rug. Instead he was bracing himself, holding his arm in position, his hand no more than six inches from Syd's knee.

Then, almost imperceptibly, he allowed a space to develop between two of those long curved fingers which had measured out the trauma of World War Two in Beethoven's piano sonatas.

As if his own hand were being nudged towards Morgan's, Syd watched the joint pass smoothly between them. And although Morgan lifted it to his lips as if it might be about to go off in his face, he drew and inhaled efficiently enough, without any undue popping of his eyes, and he was in no hurry to expel the smoke.

'It really is quite mild,' was his eventual verdict, using the same adjective he had applied to his stroke.

'But do we observe the correct protocols? Should one pass from left to right or right to left?' He paused. 'Although with only two partakers, I imagine it amounts to much the same thing – '

Either way, he did not hand the joint back immediately.

After it had passed between them twice more, Syd spoke.

'The American artist I told you about,' he said, 'the one who was shot at? He apparently said something this year about *floruits* –

'That in the future fame will be ever more fleeting. That in the end everyone will be world famous for fifteen minutes.'

Morgan rocked with a more mellow version of his signature little sneeze of amusement.

'Only fifteen minutes?'

Syd shrugged.

'It would have an appeal,' Morgan said. 'He is suggesting a form of Buggins' turn? A quarter of an hour before the mast, then a great deal of pottering about to fill all the other unforgiving minutes.'

Syd sniffed.

'I'm sure you've done more than just potter about since 1924.'

'Oh? No, mostly pottering – I would have to say.

'There has been the odd volume of non-fiction, some journalism, a certain amount of broadcasting on social and political matters. I have always maintained a formidable output of correspondence too, although latterly I have had to dictate.

'And of course, in the time-honoured tradition, when it comes to creativity I have addressed the public at some length on just how to do what I myself no longer find it possible to do!'

Syd flashed a smile.

'One has also felt compelled to speak out on behalf of other writers,' Morgan went on, 'and in defence of freedom of speech in general, as with the *Lady Chatterley* Trial – '

'You spoke at that?'

Like any forward fourteen-year-old, Syd would have been aware in 1960 of the public furore when Penguin Books was found not guilty of a breach of the new Obscene Publications

Act in publishing the late D H Lawrence's final novel.

'It was important to champion him,' Morgan answered. 'Lawrence was the greatest imaginative novelist of my generation.'

Impressed, Syd grinned slowly and perhaps a little shyly.

'So it's you we've got to thank for the permissive society?'

'Oh! Given that I was just one of thirty-five "expert" witnesses, that is a somewhat extreme claim.' But he looked not entirely displeased that Syd should have made it. A sly smile crept across his face.

'We all may have wondered how many of us Lawrence would have defended in return, had he been in a position to. But one must not carp, for where would we all be without him – or, more properly, his work?

'It is always the work, d'you see – making its way out there in the world, the genie outside of the bottle –

'As for the permissive society, there is no telling how much longer such a thing may last. Future prospects are uncertain on so many fronts. The human race does seem to be advancing to disaster via vulgarity.'

He took a moment, as though to reassess what he'd just said.

'One does need a certain amount of vulgarity, I accept. The little dash of filth without which the composite spirit cannot cohere.

'But even so – '

Syd narrowed his eyes and picked at his lower lip, seeming in two minds whether to follow up what may have been only a tangential point for Morgan.

'I'm not at all well read,' he decided to say in the end, 'and I may have this completely wrong, but didn't you write a short story about the future? – '

Morgan dipped his head.

'Post-apocalyptic, a failing future world?' he asked Syd back. 'Or at least the future as imagined some sixty years ago. Yes I did. Go on.'

'Well, I just remember being struck by the boy in it. A boy and his mother. They were living apart, in air-conditioned underground cells at opposite ends of the earth. Isolation cells – '

He shrugged and Morgan reached for the joint.

'You were struck in what way?'

'Well, I know it's probably perverse. But I kind of envied them.'

'Envied?'

'Being in places where they couldn't be got at. And there was music – piped into the cells at the flick of a switch. And people could share their ideas – ideas about art – via telescreens – '

Morgan studied him.

'This is a picture of a future that attracts you?'

'No, well I – No, as I say – I don't suppose you meant it to be taken literally. But I do remember thinking it mightn't be so bad. An existence like that.

'It seemed like, perhaps, a possible solution.'

'For the world?'

Syd smiled down at his feet.

'For me. Of course it felt wrong, but it also felt – as if it might be safe. Secure.'

He turned a flushed smile on Morgan.

'The way it feels in here.'

Morgan offered him back the joint.

'But here you are not in isolation, Roger,' he pointed out. 'Or should that still, for at least a short while longer, be Syd?'

Noticing that there was perhaps only one more hit to be had from the joint, Syd let his hand waver but Morgan made him take it.

'You are not in isolation,' he repeated, and he cast his old arm in an arc at the room. 'We are with you. We all are. Comradeship!'

With the joint extinguished, Syd carefully fed its remains into the matchbox lined with ash, which he then closed up.

Again Morgan put out a hand.

'I shall keep it as a memento,' he told Syd, taking it from him.

'Although when I look at it tomorrow, I shall probably have only the dimmest idea where I got it from. I spoke the truth to you before. For many years now I have not been, as a rule, this – competent. As you will have sensed from my muddle when first I woke to find you.'

Reflexively Syd felt for his neck chain.

'Yes, you – Well, I can understand why that was.

'But at the very start it was as if you weren't just afraid – I mean, from what you cried out, you also seemed to recognise me?'

Morgan smiled down at the matchbox he was thoughtfully studying.

'Afraid?' he repeated, as if this surprised him. 'And yet – yes, there was some fear. At least until my confusion cleared.'

'Can I ask, though – ' Syd persisted. 'Do you remember – Can I ask who you thought I was?'

With his smile still in place, and his eyes still on the matchbox, Morgan flinched at the recollection.

'It was such an oddly vivid sensation. Odd in the sense that long ago I wrote of such a moment, but I had not until today experienced it myself.

'I felt a sharp pain dart through my head, making me conscious of the exact form of my eye sockets.

'Then it was as if I were being made to see the whole of everything at once – '

He broke off and Syd sat forward on the *pouffe*, taking him almost within reaching distance of Kenneth Grahame's book on the floor.

'Everything?' he asked.

'There was a figure directly in front of me.'

Morgan made a gesture back towards where Syd had been standing.

'It was of course you, but it was also the godson I lost, and still again it was my own young lost father. All of you – as it were, conflated.'

'And that made you afraid –?'

In asking, Syd went forward on to his knees to pick up the spilled book, then he sat back on his heels holding it horizontally before Morgan in both hands, small though it was, like an offertory plate. It could have looked inattentive or even impolite to combine his question with the action. Syd himself frowned as if unsure why he had felt so impelled.

'No,' Morgan replied. 'It wasn't that.

'There was another behind you – larger, older, fading back

into my dreams as he brought you forward. He seemed to be – presenting you.

'And forgive an old man's fancy, but for a moment I believed I could see upon this other figure a bearded mouth with a half-smile at its corners, the curve of shaggy limbs –

'The one I felt unable to face was him. Unable and – after all this time – unworthy. That particular friend and helper.'

Morgan half-smiled.

His eyes had been closed as he spoke. On opening them he saw what Syd was holding before him and the beatific nod he gave in acknowledgement was, this time, one of true recognition.

For in the seventh chapter of this book, the two riverside creatures find the Otter's son nestling fast asleep upon an island in the stream between the hooves of his saviour: a figure left unnamed by the author, but whose every feature and accoutrement suggests him to be Pan the goat god, who has guided the comrades towards him with his music.

Morgan reached out, though not to take Grahame's book from Syd but in order to push it back more securely into his lost-and-found guest's possession.

For half a moment their three hands were together on the binding, and the music of the silent room seemed to crest then fall away.

'I wish,' said Syd, 'I could have seen him too – '

Morgan looked at him. 'But you very well may have.'

Syd began to shake his head but Morgan wouldn't have it.

'Your person at the BBC?' he suggested impishly. 'Was

that not him too, or an aspect of him, projected among us? Since, as we know, one cannot look with mortal eye upon things rightly kept hidden – '

Syd turned his face to the hearth and Morgan nearly giggled.

'My dearest boy,' he cried, 'he sent you!'

Both of them studied the fire as the room's silence deepened, each lost in his own thoughts until Morgan in a flurry of good-natured wheezing and groaning broke the spell by wrestling himself out of the armchair and up on to his feet.

He looked none too stable at first but soon enough got his bearings.

Meanwhile Syd pressed Grahame's book to his breast with one hand and with the other pushed himself upright too. He hovered close to Morgan's elbow, ready to intervene again if required.

'My steamed lemon curd roll will be waiting,' Morgan announced, 'along with all the rest of it – '

As he spoke he looked about him in the room, as if assessing in which direction he should now strike out. Distractedly he glanced at the matchbox in his hand before holding it up at Syd like a tiny trophy and slipping it into his trouser pocket with a smile.

Then he rapped a knuckle on the book Syd was holding.

'I should like you to have it,' he said. 'One token of remembrance in return for another. Of a day we are unlikely to know again!'

Syd stared, lost for words, as Morgan continued to cast about himself.

'But – ' Syd managed finally to say. 'But I can't take this book.

'It must be so awfully valuable – And well, it's part of your collection – '

Morgan moved away even as Syd was speaking, heading with a highly cautious step towards the landing door, beside which he had spotted what he was looking for: his voluminous academic gown dumped in a heap on a small occasional table.

'If you would like the book, it is yours.'

Syd stalked after him across the floor, emphatically setting down the book on the mantelpiece as he went.

Morgan, having slung his gown over his left shoulder with stiff-armed panache, turned to Syd and noticed his empty hands.

'It's – It's so kind of you,' the younger man said, shaking his head. 'I really am most obliged. But I – Those stories meant the world to me once. But perhaps – I wonder if perhaps now I shouldn't look quite so much to the past – ?'

'As you wish, entirely as you wish – '

'And besides,' Syd persevered, 'it's not a very fair exchange. A first-edition *Wind in the Willows* for a matchbox full of ash.'

He smiled, but a sterner expression briefly contorted Morgan's features.

'Are you forgetting,' he asked, 'that I may already have had something of yours?'

Syd's face flared.

'Something for which, I admit,' Morgan added, 'I may at the time have paid a small sum.'

'You have it?' asked Syd in a hushed voice.

'My painting?'

*

Morgan plumped up the fabric of the garment over his shoulder. Even in the doorway's gloom Syd would have been able to see several greasy food stains streaking it.

'The word I used was "may",' Morgan stopped just short of chastising him. 'And while I may once have had it, I may also since have moved it on.'

He was looking past Syd, scanning the room once again like a shopper making his thorough inspection of all the displayed apples.

'But as far as you are concerned,' he said, 'where that painting now happens to be is of little consequence.'

He put a hand on Syd's arm, possibly to steady himself before repeating with a sudden access of vigour something he had said before:

'We throw forth our work to the world, and there it must have its own life! The genie, d'you see, that genie –

'You might even perhaps regard this as laying up treasure in eternity, since a thing of beauty is of course a joy forever!'

Syd made no reply.

'You have just told me, too, that you prefer not to look back. At your age, and in your circumstances, that would seem to me to be wise.'

He leaned in and exerted more pressure on Syd's sleeve.

'And you can always draw yourself some more flies, can you not?'

Syd's face threatened to fall but as if to prevent it he raised his chin.

'However you came to be here,' Morgan told him, 'I

submit that it was not to retrieve a piece of property.

'I think I guessed this much quite soon. But you must not leave empty-handed.'

He waved across at the room's corner.

'Would you go to my desk?'

Syd didn't move at once. He looked as if he hadn't yet taken on board the full import of everything Morgan had just told him. Not that he seemed about to take issue. He may not even have heard Morgan's last request.

'Please,' the old man said, raising his voice. 'Go to my desk over there.'

Syd stirred as if from a daydream.

He crossed the room, pushed back under the desk the chair he had earlier drawn out then turned to await further instruction.

'The little bird,' Morgan called over. 'Please take my little bird.

'As I mentioned, there is a pair. In the absence of a sparrow to give to you, I should very much like to think of him by your side instead, when soon – once again – you take wing.'

Syd looked from the budgerigar to Morgan, and from Morgan to the budgerigar.

He took up the tiny uncaged creature with consummate care and putting its defiant breast to his lips, he kissed it.

Then, equally carefully, he put it back down.

'Thank you so much,' he said. 'But you really need give me nothing. Nothing in addition.'

'In addition to what?'

'To everything you've said.'

A bloom came into Syd's cheeks and he made himself smile.

'About the bucket. Everything – '

With one hand thrust in his jacket pocket, Morgan shook his head. His smile was almost as shy as Syd's.

'Well, you have been most welcome,' he replied, turning away to open the door which let in fresh blasts of evening air from the landing.

'Most welcome.

'And you might perhaps,' he said over his shoulder, 'place the little guard in front of the fire as you come.'

In the darkness outside, Morgan looked different.

Syd blinked hard as he watched him close the door to his room without a view but with vistas of infinity, then rather laboriously lock it. There was now a black-and-white checked cloth cap on his head, which he had pulled down quite low on his brow.

'Where did you get that hat?' asked Syd.

Morgan patted his jacket pocket in reply.

With his owlish spectacles, swelling belly and droopy moustache he looked less like a sage chronicler of the human condition than the kind of antique assistant found haunting the darker corners of an ironmongery. And the gown he had slung so carelessly over his shoulder, betokening perhaps how lightly he wore his great learning, could now have been seen as a soiled overall on its way to the wash.

Whatever led him to make the gesture, Syd took Morgan's elbow after the older man had shuffled over to the top of the flight of stairs.

Although there was a rail which Morgan gripped as they began to descend, Syd did not let him go. And at the first turning he released him, only to slide his arm fully through Morgan's then hold him even closer.

*

Their silent progress wasn't quick.

No one else was on hand to see them go. But if they'd been observed, Tenniel's *Looking-Glass* drawing of the old White Knight from almost exactly a century before might again have been called to mind – the older fellow apparently now being supported by this new tumble-haired Alice, although in fact he was still, in his way, escorting his younger charge ever closer to the safer reaches of the wood.

Neither man spoke before they emerged through the staircase's outer arch into their corner of the college's vast front court. The moon, just past full, was rising at its opposite side.

They stood together and watched it: first a pale yellow blur, then triangular, then round.

'I should like to know so much more about what goes on up there,' said Morgan in a small voice. 'The galaxies, the origins of man – '

He seemed to hesitate before going on.

'There is always room for a new star in the firmament,' he said as if in confidence.

Syd narrowed his eyes at the skies. 'Like a comet?'

'Like a comet? Yes – perhaps. One of the long-haired stars.'

'Is that how you see them?'

'Not I, but others have. We have the name, d'you see, from the Greek *kometes*: "long-haired".

'Your stars, my stars – '

He lowered his gaze to the mighty Chapel reaching up so gorgeously.

'There is a relatively newly acquired Rubens over there,' he told Syd in the same hushed tone. 'Very fine. An *Adoration of the Magi*.'

He paused, but only briefly.

'As a musician,' he went on, his voice sounding paler and breathier by the moment, 'you may know of the underground passage that is said to run from the Chapel all the way to Grantchester?'

Syd assented.

The story went that a fiddler set out to walk this passage's length while playing his instrument, the sound of which was finally lost to all who listened at its far end, as then was the fiddler himself, forever.

'Having grown up in this city, you know a little of the colleges?' Morgan asked. 'Your father will have been a member of one?'

'Pembroke,' said Syd, their arms still linked at the top of the short flight of outside steps.

He motioned with his head in the direction of Trumpington Street to the college where, but a fraction of a mile away, Arthur Max Barrett had in 1928 arrived on a state scholarship to begin the lacquering of his own legend, leading finally – among other recognitions – to a conference room at Addenbrooke's Hospital being named in his honour.

Under the peak of his cap, Morgan was still eyeing the Chapel's highest levels. 'Then you may be aware too of Ramsay's tragic leap?'

Again Syd made clear he did. Shortly after his own tenth

birthday, talk of the troubled King's College Dean throwing himself from the Chapel roof had electrified the city.

'The poor goose,' Morgan panted, confident enough now in both Syd and his state of mind to speak openly of a third party's suicide, and perhaps at last content to have passed on all that he felt he needed to.

The old gentleman swung his head to look left along the darkening westward path which led down to the river. Then he turned to his and Syd's immediate right to take in the more warmly lit porter's lodge to the east, on the far side of which lay the bustle of King's Parade.

He placed his free hand over Syd's wrist.

'Go east, young man!' he said.

For a moment Morgan seemed caught in his own reveries. Finally he disengaged his arm and turned to face Syd.

'I am not saying you should not come to see me another time. Unchaperoned, as it were. You would be welcome. But I very much suspect you would not then find me so capable of locking conversational horns with you.

'This has, in its way, been a kind of miracle.'

His voice quavered, and though he was looking up at Syd, the cap's peak obscured his eyes.

'It's possible – ' Syd answered. 'It's possible that another time I might not be quite this capable either. It's been – I feel I've had a kind of reprieve as well.'

Still Morgan's eyes could not be seen.

'You've been,' Syd told him, 'very good.'

Morgan chortled.

'But what else are the old for,' he asked, pausing to get his breath, 'if not to be good to the young? I am sure you will do exactly the same fifty, sixty, seventy years hence – ' He grimaced. 'After you have been dubbed Sir Roger Barrett. "For services to psychedelia"!'

The visitor gave a rueful nod.

'More likely Sir Syd, I'd think.'

'If that is to be how you are remembered.'

Beyond the college walls a clock collected its strength and struck the new hour. Gowned undergraduates streamed past in either direction at the foot of the short flight of steps. Each one seemed to be swimming very much with the tide of his own being but a few, detecting traces of dope smoke on Syd and Morgan, slowed to glance up at them before moving on – while someone else, younger still, stood in a long dark overcoat twenty steps away in the shadows just beyond the porter's lodge, biding his time and watching with a passion all his own.

Morgan blew out air in shallow little puffs to keep his breathing under control. His stoop looked more pronounced.

With a hesitant hand, Syd reached out and took the liberty of smoothing back some flailing strands of the old gentleman's hair that his cap – which ideally, like his trousers, could have been a size bigger – had caused to poke out over his right ear.

Morgan did then meet his eye, with strong emotion showing in his features. And he leaned in and kissed Syd's cheek with such ferocity that he seemed to bounce away after planting it.

In the tenderness of the moment neither man looked sure how to proceed. Footballers hugged in public in 1968; other grown men did not. But if a musical note had been sparked by their brief contact, it would have matched the joyous bark of Kenneth Grahame's Otter when at last he is reunited with his headstrong and over-ambitious wandering child.

Syd put out his hand. Morgan grasped it.

'Comradeship,' Morgan said with their palms pressed together and thumbs locked, a man who on the eve of World War Two had proclaimed that if ever he had to betray either his country or his friend, he hoped he would have the guts to betray his country.

'It is our calling, Roger,' he said with a blink of his milky eyes, 'to bring a little gaiety to the nation. I cannot say why it is the likes of us, but it is. Somewhere along the line there must be a selection, a setting apart of the goats from the sheep.'

Summoning more breath, he gripped Syd's wrist with his free hand.

'We flit in and out. Like Bede's sparrow. Like the mayfly. Strutting and fretting our hour upon the stage. A very old and down-at-heel mayfly in my own case – '

He launched into his little laugh but it turned into a cough.

'We poor things may be of the moment,' he managed to conclude, 'but the work shines on.' Then his grip on Syd's wrist grew tighter. 'And one does not want to feel, later in life, that one has not fully come off.'

As he let Syd go, Morgan's expression seemed to turn inward, a man exchanging a glance of disquiet with himself.

Softly Syd clapped him on the shoulder.

'Old comrade,' he said. 'Thank you.'

There was a distinct trembling in the aged gentleman's lower lip. He leaned in a short way and lowered his voice.

'Stand for all you are worth in the sun!' he said.

With a tiny snatched smile he touched his cap in farewell, turned, and went his way.

Syd strode off with his Tiggerish bounce and had he been able, he would surely have turned to give Morgan a final salutation before reaching the porter's lodge with its spectral figures going about their Saturday evening business.

He would very likely have turned almost at once, but he was not given that chance.

For just at the point when the presiding demigod of Saturday afternoon smiled in appreciation of his successor's handiwork while buttoning his mackintosh in readiness to leave, the young person who had been biding his time in the shadows of King's front court lurched forward.

Under one arm he held a large square object; with his free hand he was rootling around in his overcoat pocket.

And before Syd could step into the light cast from the lodge or even think about turning to wave to Morgan, the other spoke.

'Mr Barrett – '

The two lesser deities up in the clear empyrean peered closer, the face of Pan's counterpart all consternation. For lesser deities cannot know everything, which at times seems to add a little welcome spice, and Pan had a reputation for not always paying the closest attention to detail when mounting epiphanies for those in his pastoral care.

They watched as Syd too was taken unawares, skittering closer to the wall as the other made directly for him. He was maybe even about to put up a hand to ward off a possible assailant.

But there was no cause for alarm, either in the world of Morgan and Syd, or in that which oversaw it. It was twelve years too soon for this music's first martyrdom, when – just a short walk across Manhattan from where Andy Warhol, the artist Syd had talked about, managed to avoid death by assassination – it would be a primary god from Syd's own pantheon, the forty-year-old John Lennon, who would be gunned down.

Yet Syd Barrett had neither disappointed nor offended this fan.

He was confronted only by the ponytailed college servant: the awed but adroit lad who, after clocking off from his duties, had rushed home to fetch the pristine sleeve of his own copy of Pink Floyd's first album and now, producing not a gun but a biro from his pocket, mutely he asked Syd to oblige him by putting his name to *The Piper at the Gates of Dawn*.

In answering silence Syd took the pen and inscribed his *nom de plume* above an image of all four original Pink Floyd members whose linked silhouettes formed the shape of an outlandish composite creature, recalling the Grimm Brothers' tale of the town musicians of Bremen.

This was all he was required to do.

Gratified, the lad stepped aside to let Syd walk on. And

when Syd did look back to take his leave, Morgan had already shuffled on to wherever he was next expected, and vanished from view.

With under two miles to walk to his family home, Syd stalked back down the centre of King's Parade, past the ornate stone screen dividing the college from the pavement and on into Trumpington Street. People still noticed him, but against the new dark backdrop he perhaps seemed less exotic, less unlikely to be seen stitched into the night's fabric.

At the approach to the junction with Silver Street, he was moved to tilt back his head to inspect the frosty glories of the constellations – and taking his cue, the goat god above put his pipe to his lips.

A capricious little breeze danced across Syd's upturned face to blow the last of his tears dry. Then on the boy marched with freshly seeded hope, and with each step his memory faded of all that had happened since he'd run his Austin Mini aground down by the river.

In later decades it would be said, possibly too often, that anyone who remembered the 1960s hadn't really been there. The breath of kindly Pan, which cleansed as well as quickened, had more than a little to do with that – for no unsettling traces of his interventions have ever been permitted to linger in the memories of those he has helped and inspired.

As Syd entered the last long stretch of his autumn journey, along Hills Road itself, he was welcomed by the sound of a train slackening into the eel-like station platform over to the east. On the rise which took a queue of cars bumper-to-bumper across the railway lines he lengthened his stride, and the roaring tides of night received him.

THE STORY CONTINUES

Less than two years later, in June 1970, Morgan Forster died peacefully at the marital home in Coventry of former policeman Bob Buckingham, his most loyal and lasting lover. Morgan's posthumous novel *Maurice*, followed by *The Life to Come and Other Stories* – works in which for the first time he openly explored homosexual themes – served only to enhance his status as one of his century's most fondly regarded writers.

By the time of Morgan's death, Syd Barrett had all but completed the recording of a host of new tracks running a gamut from exquisite to visceral, many of them driven by lyrics of a haunted, beguiling immediacy.

The studio sessions were fitful, the musicianship often lacking in polish and sounding jaggedly "unplugged" before its time, but in early 1970 Syd's first solo long-player *The Madcap Laughs* was released, and it included an adaptation and setting of the poem 'Golden Hair' from the 25-year-old James Joyce's 1907 collection *Chamber Music*. This was succeeded in the same year by a second album, *Barrett*, with a setting of Syd's Hilaire Belloc pastiche 'Effervescing Elephant' as its final track. Eighteen years later a third collection, *Opel*, appeared, containing alternative recordings and hitherto unreleased material from 1968 to 1970.

Together these three records turned out to be – for those

who love them – unparalleled in English popular or any other music, while the sleeve of *Barrett* featured Syd's own drawing of mounted insects.

Although this was Syd's musical swansong, further visual art would follow, for upon finally travelling back to his mother's home in Cambridge from London in the early 1970s (some say on foot), and kept afloat in part by Pink Floyd royalties channelled through his former bandmates, he privately produced and later destroyed many works.

It was not all plain sailing. Syd found himself no life-partner, in ageing unglamorously he moved far away from his own gilded youth, and he was written off too readily in his reclusiveness as a burned-out casualty. Yet his comet, like Morgan's, had a very long tail and well before he died of pancreatic cancer in July 2006 at sixty years of age, many, including David Bowie and Marc Bolan, had declared a significant artistic debt to Syd Barrett's sound, his look and his constant quest for the new.

Meanwhile the group he once led lived on.

Pink Floyd's official website suggested in 2018 that "though the Floyd's Barrett era only lasted three years, it always informed what they became". Between early 1968 (when briefly before Syd's departure they were a five-piece) and the group's final disbandment in 2014, Roger Waters, David Gilmour, Rick Wright and Nick Mason formed one of the most iconic and influential ensembles in popular music history, bestriding a rock world they had done much to build and selling over 250 million records.

On the fiftieth anniversary of the release of their first

album *The Piper at the Gates of Dawn*, London's Victoria & Albert Museum mounted a multi-media retrospective of their entire career and in a recorded interview shown at this exhibition Roger Waters freely admitted that without Syd Barrett they would never have achieved their original traction.

For a group whose ethos served as a pan-generational church, Syd truly was the messiah who didn't die. Much of Pink Floyd's most resonant work since 1968 – *Wish You Were Here*, *Dark Side of the Moon*, *The Wall* – can be seen as an elegy to their beloved old comrade who still held them in a kind of thrall (notably in the extended song-suite '**S**hine On **Y**ou Crazy **D**iamond'), or else as an indirect response to their own experience of Syd, his issues and his aura before they lost all personal contact with him.

It is not recorded that Syd Barrett
ever met E M Forster – on this earth.